The Golden PICTURE DICTIONARY

By Lucille Ogle and Tina Thoburn
Illustrated by Hilary Knight

A GOLDEN BOOK • NEW YORK
Western Publishing Company, Inc., Racine, Wisconsin 53404

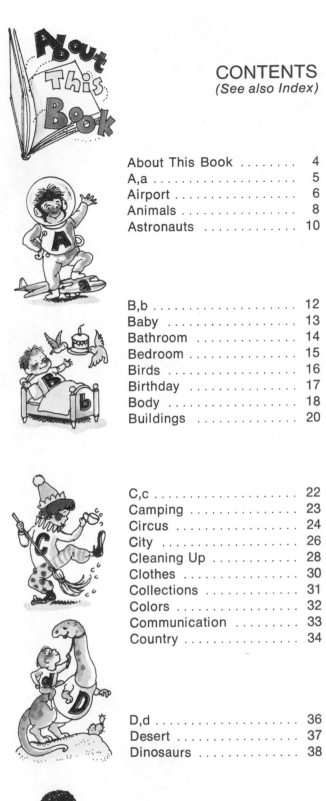

CONTENTS
(See also Index)

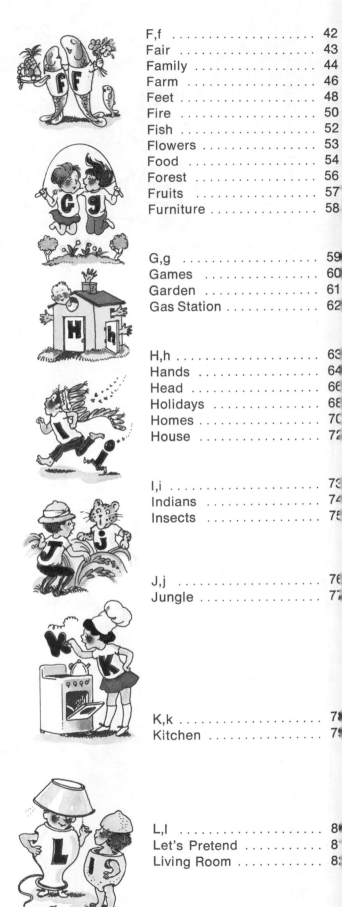

The Golden Picture Dictionary has been designed especially for young children who are just beginning to explore the exciting meanings and sounds and printed forms of their language. Its purpose is to help them acquire knowledge about more than twenty-five hundred words and the ways these words are used in understanding and communicating about people, places, objects, actions, feelings, and relationships.

It is our belief that the most effective means of helping beginners learn about words is to involve them in enjoyable activities that lead them to *use* the words. Accordingly, we have organized a majority of the words selected for inclusion in the book into eighty-three natural categories and built around them a variety of identification, matching, classification, and comparison games.

The broad scope of categories and the delightful art by Hilary Knight aim to capture the interest of every child. A ride in the country, a city street, a visit to the pet shop—and scenes to stretch the imagination: what goes on underground, different kinds of families. Future homemakers will find information about food, clothing, shopping, and caring for the house. Those interested in science and technology will learn about astronauts and modes of communication and transportation. The budding ecologist will want to contrast life in a pond community with that in the desert or forest.

For the beginning reader there are twenty-six alphabetical categories which illustrate the shapes and sounds of letters and show their proper order. Each alphabet page shows a variety of words that begin with the given letter. The sound or sounds commonly associated with each letter are clearly illustrated. For example, the *A* page contains words beginning with three different sounds—apple, apron, autograph.

Word and Category Selection

In selecting words for inclusion in this book, we started with the venerable word lists compiled by Horn, Rinsland, Thorndike, and Dolch, which are based on frequency of usage. To be sure important basic words were not left out, we checked the vocabularies used in six widely used beginning reading programs. Next, we consulted with our young friends and added a large number of the "mind-stretching" words they liked best—words they had learned from their older brothers and sisters, from television, and from children's books. Finally we picked out those words that could be illustrated with no question about their meaning.

Once the words were selected, they seemed to fall into natural categories. We were delighted to find that these categories matched the universal interests and experiences of young children. We felt that they would derive greater satisfaction and understanding from such groupings of words than from a totally alphabetical arrangement, so we organized the dictionary alphabetically *by category,* and wherever it made sense to do so, *within category.* A few of the words were repeated to help balance and round out the category and alphabet pages. An Index was added to help adults and older children quickly locate words.

Activities

To us, the most exciting feature of the book is the rich variety of learning activities it includes. Children are asked to answer questions, match pictures, compare objects, and group them in special ways. Always the goal is to help them associate words with their meanings. It is our ardent hope that every youngster who opens this book will find something in it to kindle the desire to learn.

LUCILLE OGLE
TINA THOBURN

A BCDEFGHIJKLMNOPQRSTUVWXYZ

Amy aims an arrow.

All these words begin with **A**.

abacus

accordion

acorn

alligator

alphabet

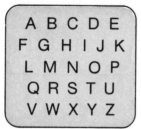

anchor

angelfish

ape

apple

apron

autograph

automobile

Are you able to think of any more **a** words?

a bcdefghijklmnopqrstuvwxyz

A
a

airport

Have you ever visited the airport?
It is a busy place.
Aircraft and people are coming and going.

runway

heliport

helicopter

waiting room

terminal

AIRPORT BUS

luggage

Find these things in the picture. How are they used?

| escalator | suitcases | television | windsock |

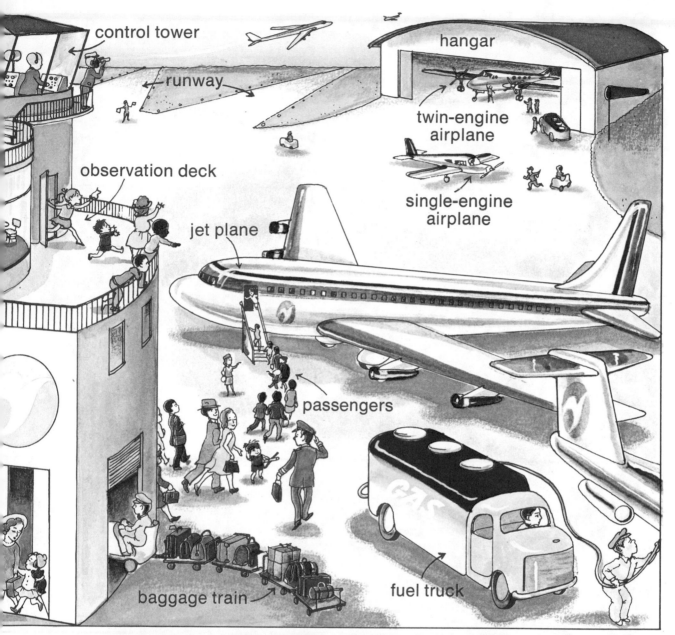

control tower

hangar

runway

twin-engine
airplane

single-engine
airplane

observation deck

jet plane

passengers

baggage train

fuel truck

Find these people in the picture. What do they do?

| pilot | porter | flight attendant | ticket agent |

A
a

animals

There are many kinds of animals.
They are different sizes, shapes, and colors.

elephant

bat

flying squirrel

monkey

giraffe

panther

porcupine

camel

moose

horse

kangaroo

mole

wolf

dogs

pigs

whale

All the animals on this page are called mammals.
Mammal babies drink milk from their mothers.

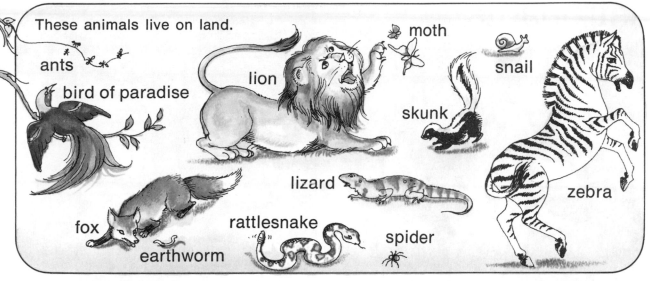

These animals live on land.

ants
bird of paradise
lion
moth
snail
skunk
zebra
lizard
fox
rattlesnake
spider
earthworm

These animals live on land and in water.

crocodile
flamingo
penguin
polar bear
salamander
seal
turtle
frog

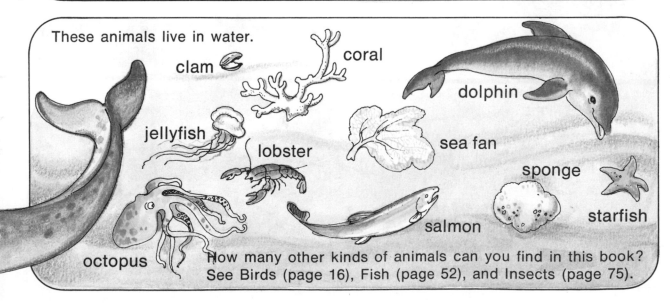

These animals live in water.

clam
coral
dolphin
jellyfish
lobster
sea fan
sponge
salmon
starfish
octopus

How many other kinds of animals can you find in this book?
See Birds (page 16), Fish (page 52), and Insects (page 75).

astronauts

Three astronauts are getting dressed for a flight in space.

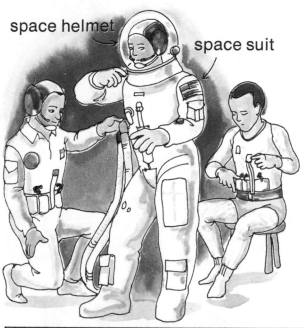

space helmet

space suit

Now they are inside their space capsule.

Men in Mission Control will help guide the space flight.

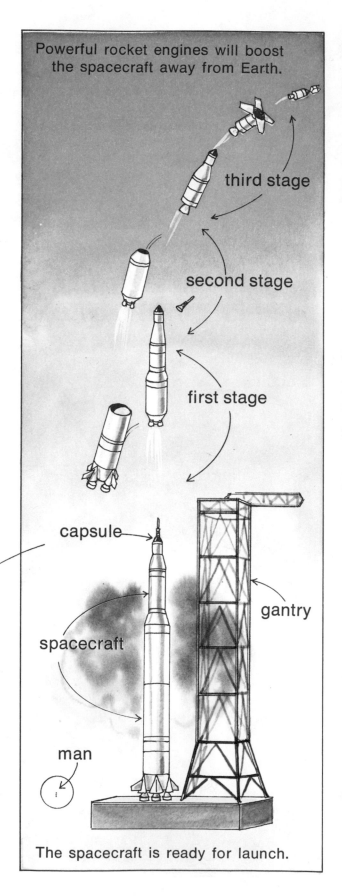

Powerful rocket engines will boost the spacecraft away from Earth.

third stage

second stage

first stage

capsule

spacecraft

gantry

man

The spacecraft is ready for launch.

The astronauts blast off into space.

They look back at Earth.

The astronauts orbit the moon.

Two astronauts land on the moon
in the lunar module.

moon rock

One astronaut waits
in the command module.

Soon his friends return.

Now all the astronauts speed
back to Earth.

They are picked up by a helicopter
and taken to a recovery ship.

The astronauts are happy
to be back on Earth.

Ben blows a big brass bugle.

A **B** CDEFGHIJKLMNOPQRSTUVWXYZ

The words below begin with **B**.

ball

balloon

bank

barrel

bell

binoculars

books

boomerang

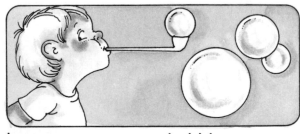

boy   bubbles

butter

button

Think of some boys' names that begin with **b**.

a **b** c d e f g h i j k l m n o p q r s t u v w x y z

baby

The Becks have a new baby.

baby

big sister

Mama

Daddy

big brother

Which of these things did you use when you were a tiny baby?

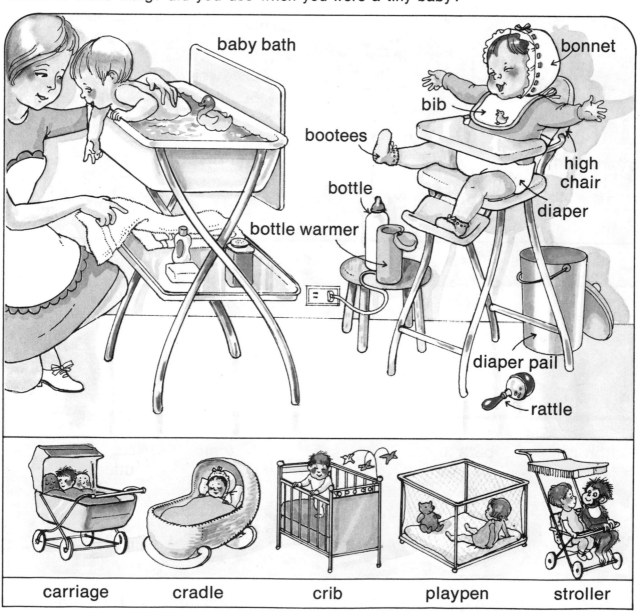

baby bath

bonnet

bib

bootees

bottle

bottle warmer

high chair

diaper

diaper pail

rattle

| carriage | cradle | crib | playpen | stroller |

13

bathroom

I take my bath in the bathroom.

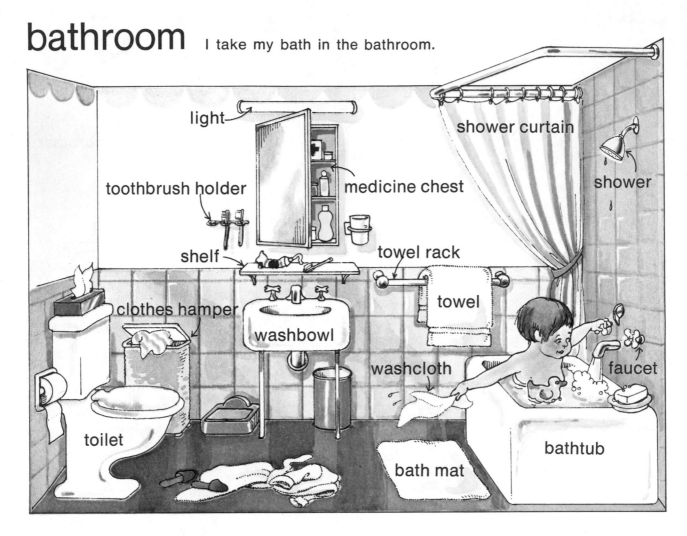

- light
- toothbrush holder
- shelf
- clothes hamper
- washbowl
- toilet
- medicine chest
- shower curtain
- shower
- towel rack
- towel
- washcloth
- faucet
- bath mat
- bathtub

Can you find these things in the bathroom?

| bathrobe | bath toy | glass | scale | soap |
| tissues | toilet paper | toothbrush | toothpaste | wastebasket |

bedroom

Each night I sleep in my bedroom.
It is quiet when the lights are out.

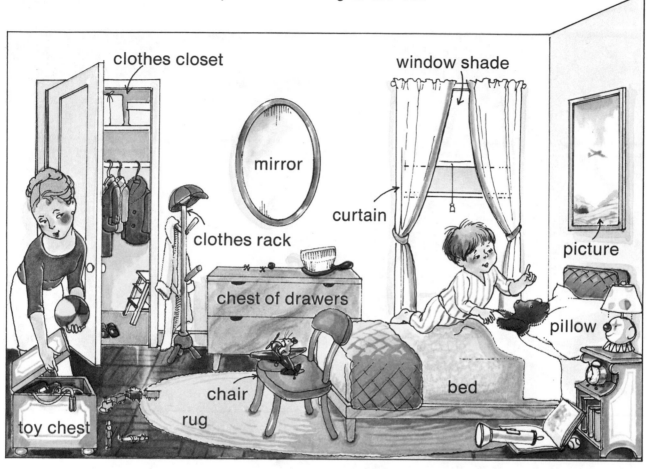

clothes closet

window shade

mirror

clothes rack

curtain

picture

chest of drawers

pillow

chair

bed

rug

toy chest

Do you have these things in your bedroom?

book

brush

clock

comb

flashlight

lamp

mirror

pogo stick

teddy bear

tricycle

birds

Birds have two wings and two legs.
Their bodies are covered with feathers.

Most birds can fly.

eagle

toucan

hummingbird

parrot

crow

woodpecker

Some birds cannot fly.

bobwhite

ostrich

pheasant

penguin

kiwi

swan

stork

Birds hatch from eggs.

robin

nest

See if you can find some more birds in this book.

birthday

Each year you have a birthday.
It is the special day you were born.

How old will you be on your next birthday?

1 year old	2 years old	3 years old	4 years old
5 years old	6 years old	7 years old	100 years old

Beth is having a birthday party.
Can you tell how old she is?

paper hat

birthday cake

candles

birthday card

present

17

B
b body

My body is covered with skin. Is yours?

My bird's body is covered with feathers.

My fish's body is covered with scales.

My cat's body is covered with fur.

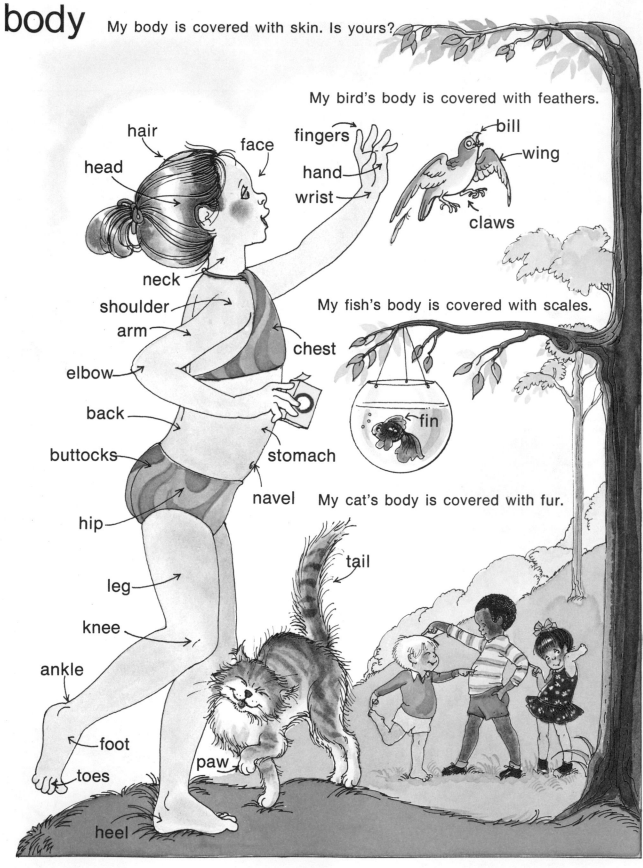

hair
face
head
fingers
bill
wing
hand
wrist
claws
neck
shoulder
arm
chest
elbow
back
fin
buttocks
stomach
navel
hip
tail
leg
knee
ankle
foot
paw
toes
heel

How many of these things can you do with your body?

climb

chin

fly

swing

slide

hang

push

fall

ride

pull

somersault

roll

crawl

dig

bounce

swim

bend

What do you wear on your body? Look on page 30.

B
b

buildings

People build many marvelous buildings.
How are these buildings used?

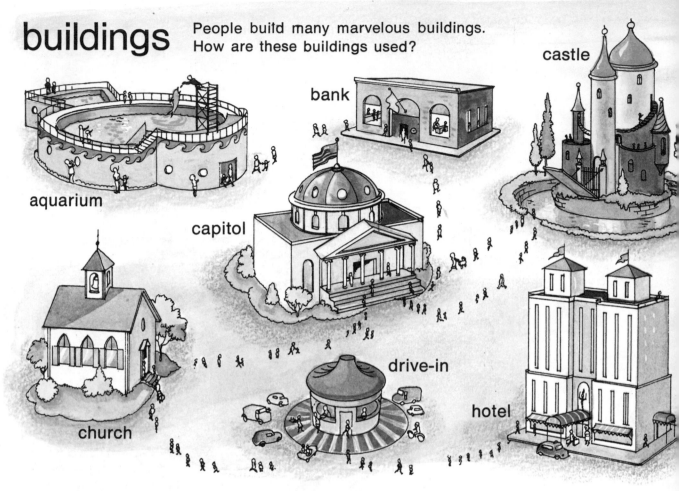

aquarium

bank

capitol

castle

church

drive-in

hotel

People use different kinds of material for their buildings.

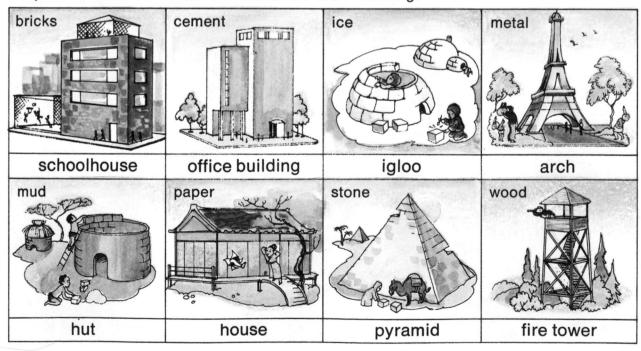

bricks	cement	ice	metal
schoolhouse	office building	igloo	arch
mud	paper	stone	wood
hut	house	pyramid	fire tower

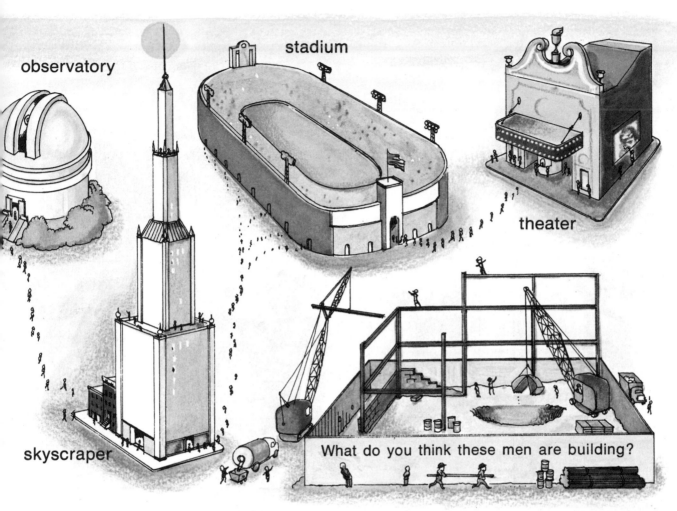

observatory

stadium

theater

skyscraper

What do you think these men are building?

Here are some materials you can use to make play buildings.

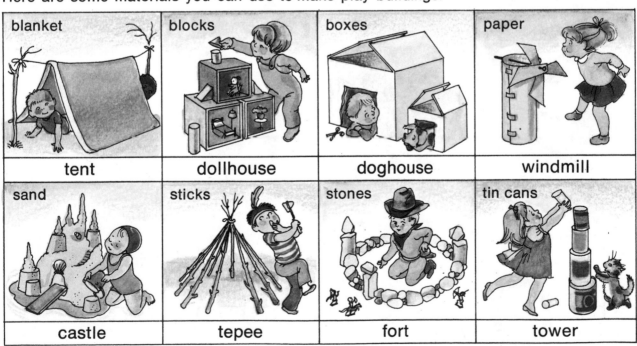

blanket	blocks	boxes	paper
tent	dollhouse	doghouse	windmill
sand	sticks	stones	tin cans
castle	tepee	fort	tower

Carlos carries a canary in a cage.

AB **C** DEFGHIJKLMNOPQRSTUVWXYZ

Here are some words that begin with **C**.

camera

cards

carrier

cat

celery

chain

children

compass

cookies

cradle

cub

cupcake

How many **C** words can you count?

ab **C** defghijklmnopqrstuvwxyz

camping

Many families like to go camping.

log cabin

hiker

tent

grill

How do campers use these things?

| campstool | canteen | charcoal | firewood | flashlight |

| frying pan | grill | hiking boots | knapsack | sleeping bag |

circus

The circus tent is sometimes called the big top.

circus band

acrobat

aerialist

bandleader

spectators

bareback rider

tightrope walker

lions

dogs and ponies

clowns

ringmaster

Here are some more circus performers.

chimpanzee   cyclist   juggler   fat lady   fire-eater

Many people and animals work together to make a circus fun.

balloon man

cotton-candy man

net

elephants

tumbler

elephant trainer

bears

seals

lion tamer

barker

human cannonball

strong man   sword swallower   tattooed man   tall man

C
c

city

Many people live and work in the city.

| bus stop | fire hydrant | mail carrier | newsboy | park bench |

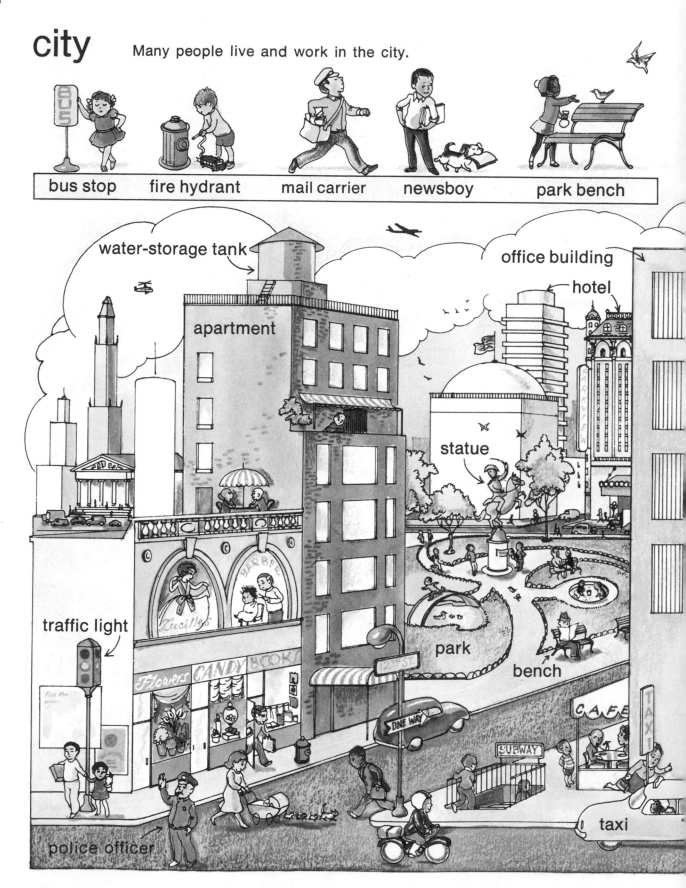

water-storage tank

office building

hotel

apartment

statue

traffic light

park

bench

police officer

taxi

Find these people and things in the picture.

police officer   riveter   statue   taxi   telephone

factory

street

sidewalk

theater

newsstand

street lamp

MAIN ST.

bus

mailbox

manhole

telephone booth

cleaning up

Which things can each person use for cleaning up?

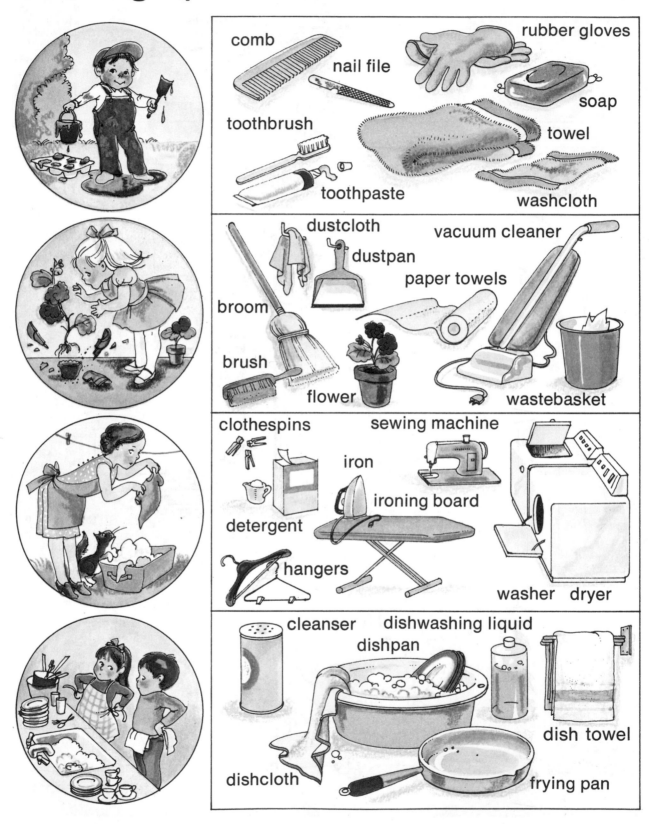

comb

nail file

rubber gloves

soap

toothbrush

towel

toothpaste

washcloth

dustcloth

dustpan

vacuum cleaner

paper towels

broom

brush

flower

wastebasket

clothespins

sewing machine

iron

ironing board

detergent

hangers

washer   dryer

cleanser   dishwashing liquid

dishpan

dish towel

dishcloth

frying pan

What cleaning equipment can these people use to make things neat and tidy?

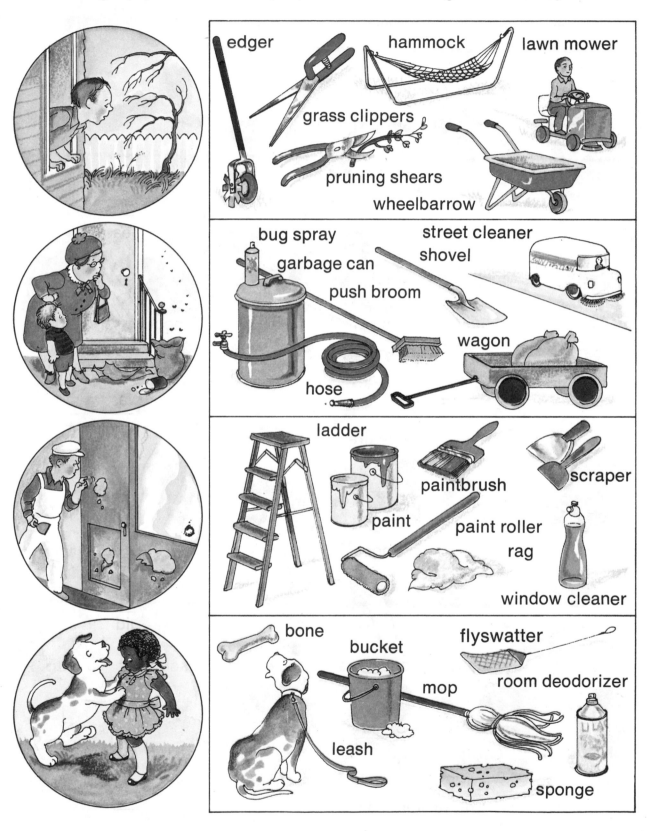

edger

hammock

lawn mower

grass clippers

pruning shears

wheelbarrow

bug spray

street cleaner

garbage can

shovel

push broom

hose

wagon

ladder

paintbrush

scraper

paint

paint roller

rag

window cleaner

bone

flyswatter

bucket

room deodorizer

mop

leash

sponge

clothes

We wear clothes to protect our bodies.
We also wear clothes to look nice.

clothes hanger

Which clothes would you wear in summer?

belt	blouse	blue jeans
boots	cap	coat
dress	hat	jacket
mittens	necktie	nightgown
overalls	panties	party dress
pajamas	raincoat	rain hat
scarf	shirt	shoes
shorts	skirt	slacks
slip	slippers	sneakers
snowsuit	socks	suit
sundress	sweater	tights
T-shirt	underpants	undershirt

Which clothes would you wear in winter?

collections

See all the wonderful collections
at the children's Hobby Show.

Bobby collects bottle caps.

Betty collects buttons.

Curt collects coins.

Dolly collects dolls.

Marvin collects marbles.

Paula collects post cards.

Ricky collects rocks.

Sheila collects shells.

Stuart collects stamps.

What kind of collection would you like to make?

C
c

colors

There are many beautiful colors in the world.

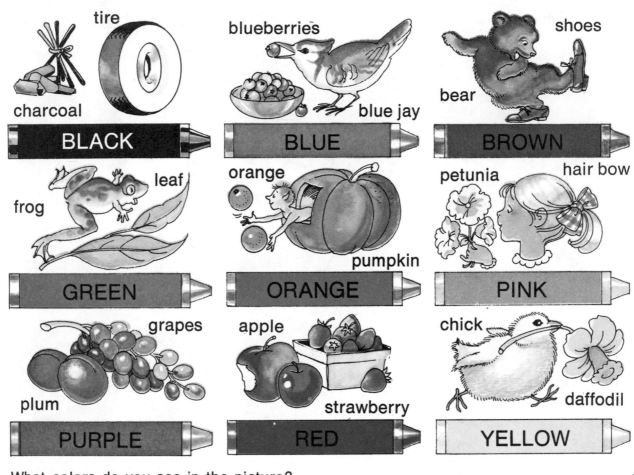

tire
charcoal
BLACK

blueberries
blue jay
BLUE

shoes
bear
BROWN

frog
leaf
GREEN

orange
pumpkin
ORANGE

petunia
hair bow
PINK

grapes
plum
PURPLE

apple
strawberry
RED

chick
daffodil
YELLOW

What colors do you see in the picture?

communication

Cathy and Colin are sending messages to each other.

They are communicating.

Cathy writes a letter.

Colin reads the letter.

Colin dials the telephone.

Cathy answers the telephone.

Here are other ways to communicate ideas.

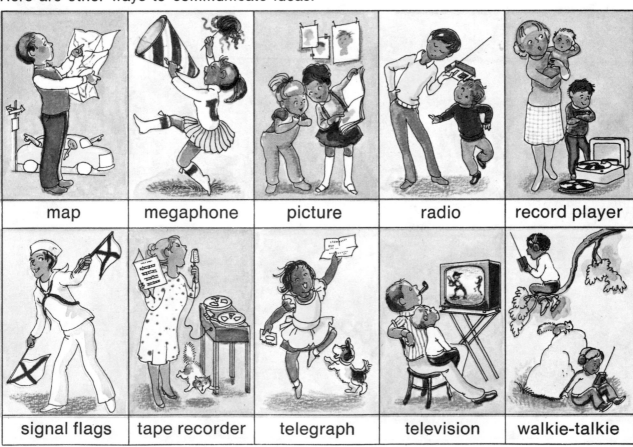

| map | megaphone | picture | radio | record player |
| signal flags | tape recorder | telegraph | television | walkie-talkie |

C
c
country

People and houses are far apart in the country.
It is usually quiet and peaceful.

woods

pastu

farm

wheat field

electric fence

cornfield

DEAD END

MILLSTONE CORNER

church

swing

WORMS

MILK

path

fishing hole

There is plenty of fresh air.

motel

freeway

clubhouse

orchard

golfers

golf course

parking lot

golf cart

stone quarry

cemetery

dirt road

mill

stream

covered bridge

roadside rest area

Diana dresses her doll.

ABC D EFGHIJKLMNOPQRSTUVWXYZ

Here are some words that begin with D.

dandelion

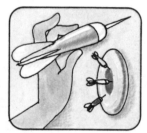

darts

dictionary

dishes

dachshund

Dalmatian

Doberman pinscher

deerhound

dogs

doormat   dragon

duck

dumbbell

Can you think of a dozen different d words?

abc d efghijklmnopqrstuvwxyz

desert

The desert is very dry land.
It is hot during the day and cold at night.

AFRICAN DESERT

date palms

sand dunes

tent

caravan

camel

sheep

oasis

nomad

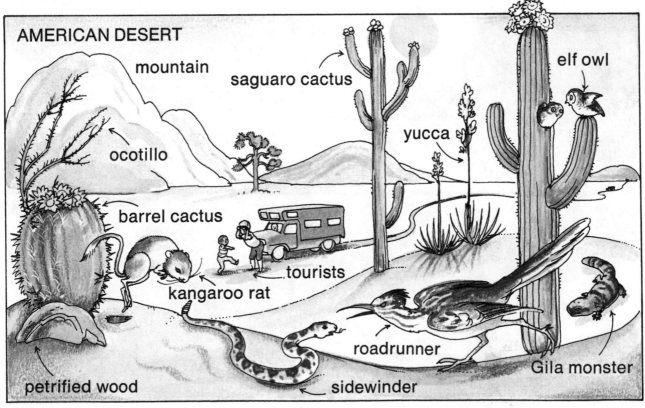

AMERICAN DESERT

mountain

saguaro cactus

elf owl

yucca

ocotillo

barrel cactus

tourists

kangaroo rat

roadrunner

Gila monster

petrified wood

sidewinder

D
d
dinosaurs

Millions of years ago reptiles called dinosaurs lived on earth.
Most dinosaurs were plant eaters.

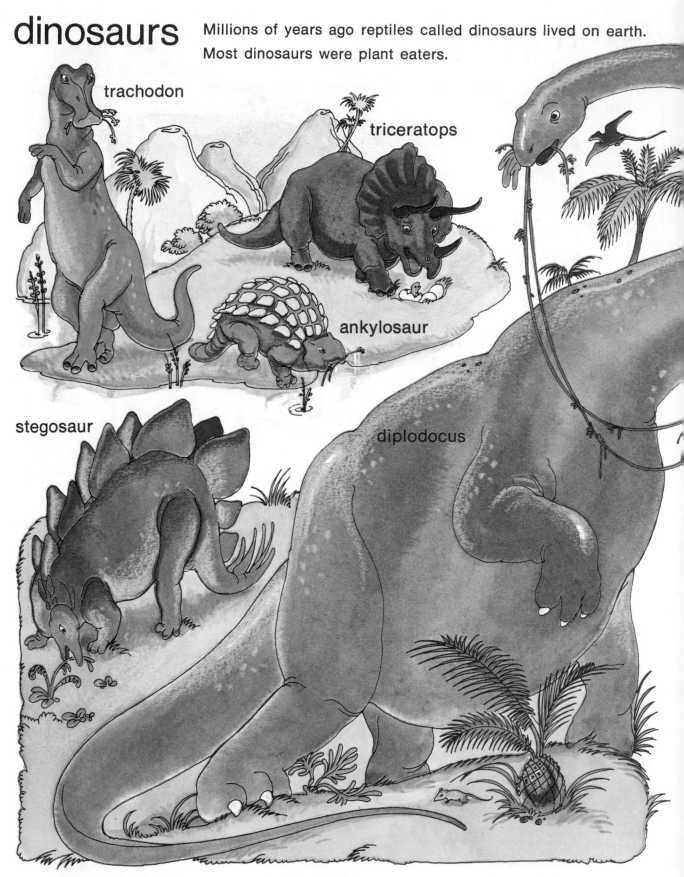

trachodon

triceratops

ankylosaur

stegosaur

diplodocus

Some dinosaurs were meat eaters.

allosaur

compsognathus

No dinosaurs live on earth today.

But we can see dinosaur fossils in some museums.

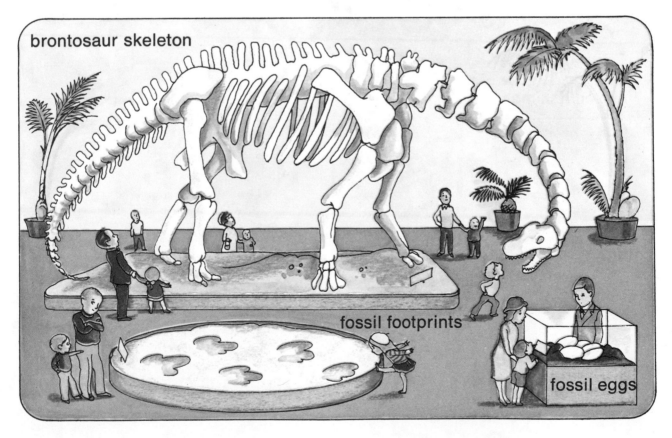

brontosaur skeleton

fossil footprints

fossil eggs

Ellen eats an egg.

ABCD **E** FGHIJKLMNOPQRSTUVWXYZ

These words begin with E.

eagle

eel

eight elephants

eleven Eskimos

elf

ermine

excavator

exercise

Did you find some words that end with e?

abcd **e** fghijklmnopqrstuvwxyz

experiments

Scientists experiment to find out about things.

First, make a collection of little things like these.

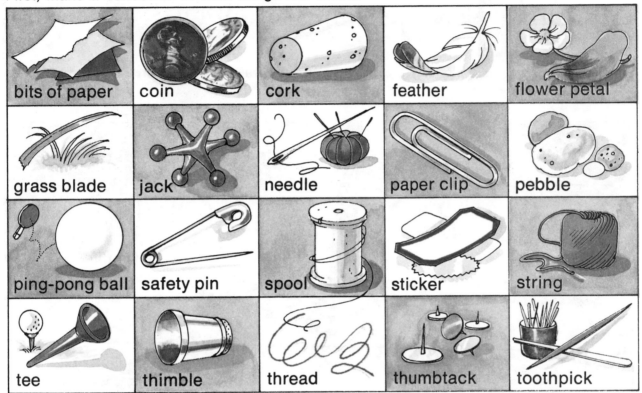

bits of paper	coin	cork	feather	flower petal
grass blade	jack	needle	paper clip	pebble
ping-pong ball	safety pin	spool	sticker	string
tee	thimble	thread	thumbtack	toothpick

You can experiment too.

See which things you can pick up with a magnet.

magnet

steel pin

Which things will float in a bowl of water?

water toy

nail

Rub a plastic comb with a wool mitten.

Which things can you pick up with the comb?

Felix finds a frog.

ABCDE **F** GHIJKLMNOPQRSTUVWXYZ

F is the first letter in each of these words.

fairy

fan   feather

fingerprints

fireflies

fish

five fat fire fighters

footprints

fort   fence

four flags flying   funnel

Can you find some more **f** words?

abcde **f** ghijklmnopqrstuvwxyz

42

fair

It's fun to go to a fair.

Here are some things you might see there.

merry-go-round

Ferris wheel

audience

contestants

blue ribbon

judge

family

People who live together form a family.

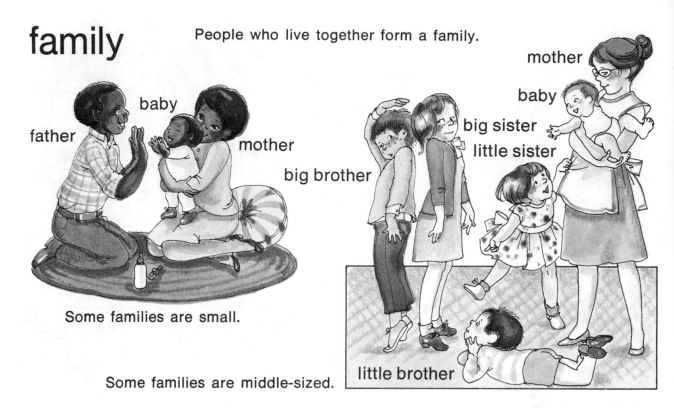

father · baby · mother

Some families are small.

big brother · mother · baby · big sister · little sister · little brother

Some families are middle-sized.

Some families are large.

father · grandfather · grandmother · brother · uncle · aunt · mother · baby · sister · cousins

How many people are in your family?

Many animals live together in family groups.

CARDINAL FAMILY

mother
father
babies

FOX FAMILY

father fox
mother vixen
young fox kits

GORILLA FAMILY

mother
father
baby
aunts
uncles

To what families do these babies belong?

bird
human
fox
gorilla

F
f
farm

Farmers raise animals and grow crops on farms.

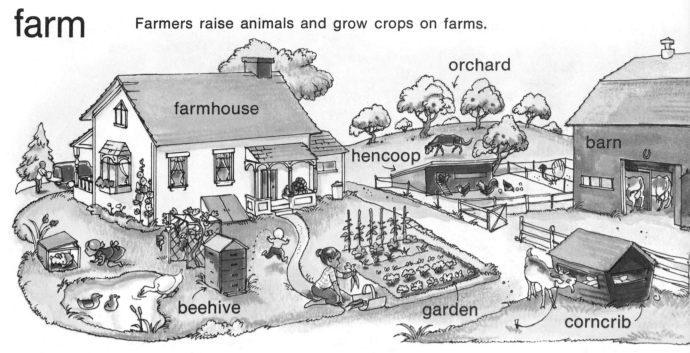

farmhouse
orchard
hencoop
barn
beehive
garden
corncrib

Name these farm animals and show where they live.

bees • chickens • cow • donkey

ducks • geese • goat • horse

pigs • rabbits • sheep • turkey

Which farm animals give us these?

butter • eggs • honey • meat • milk • wool

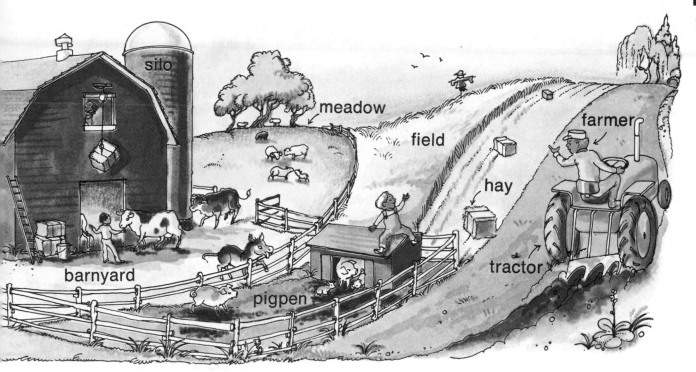

silo

meadow

field

farmer

hay

barnyard

tractor

pigpen

Crops are plants farmers grow on farms.

| corn | cotton | fruits | sugar cane | vegetables | wheat |

Which crops are used to make these?

bread   cereal   cloth   juice   salad   sugar

F f

feet

Feet are the two things at the end of our legs that help us stand up.

heel

toes

bare feet

left foot

right foot

Here are some things we wear on our feet.

baby shoes

bandage

bedroom slippers

boots

cowboy boots

Father's shoes

flip-flops

flippers

moccasins

Mother's shoes

party shoes

rubbers

sandals

school shoes

socks

tennis shoes

Here are some things we do with our feet.

dance   gallop   hop   ice-skate

jump   kick   march   pedal

roller-skate   run   ski   skip

stamp   tiptoe   walk   wiggle

Oh, look at the footprints!
Who do you think made them?

Shhh! Do you hear footsteps?

49

fire

Fire can be helpful.

Fire gives us heat.

| campfire | fireplace | furnace | hot-water heater | stove |

Fire gives us light.

| bonfire | candle | gaslight | lantern | match |

These things burn easily.

| coal | gasoline | paper | straw | wood |

These things do not burn easily.

| asbestos | bricks | fire extinguisher | glass | water |

F
f

Fire can be dangerous.
Fire fighters help fight fires.

smoke

fire

fire escape

hook

fire hose

axe

fire hydrant

rescue net

fire fighters

fire alarm box

ladder truck

megaphone

fire chief

pumper

fire engine

spotlight

firehouse dog

rescue truck

DON'T SMOKE

TAILOR

DANGER

F
f

fish

All fish are water animals. Most of them are covered with scales.

Fish have fins to help them swim.

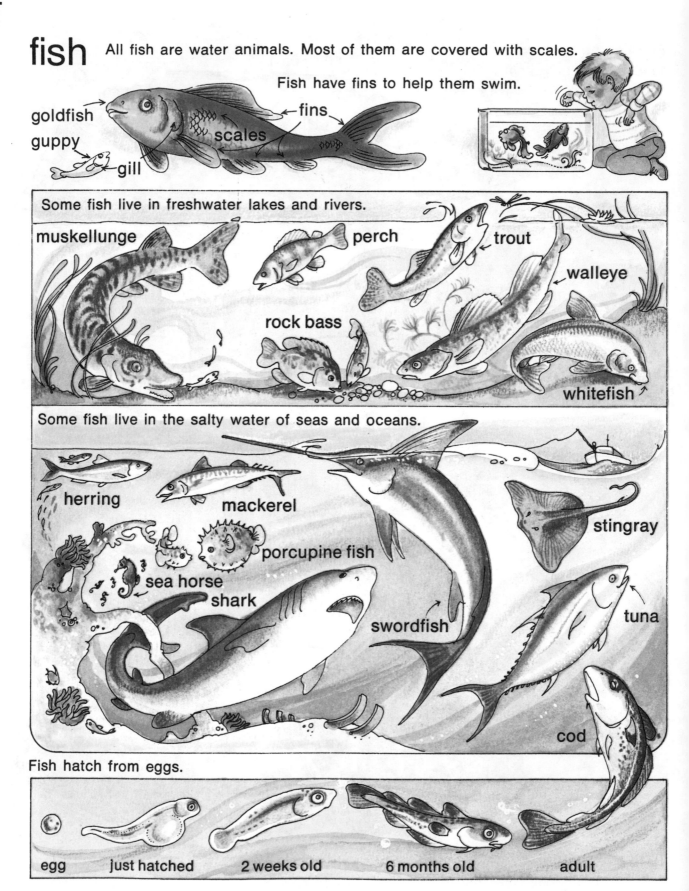

goldfish

guppy

fins

scales

gill

Some fish live in freshwater lakes and rivers.

muskellunge

perch

trout

walleye

rock bass

whitefish

Some fish live in the salty water of seas and oceans.

herring

mackerel

stingray

porcupine fish

sea horse

shark

swordfish

tuna

cod

Fish hatch from eggs.

egg · just hatched · 2 weeks old · 6 months old · adult

flowers
Many plants have beautiful flowers.

Which of these flowers are the same color?

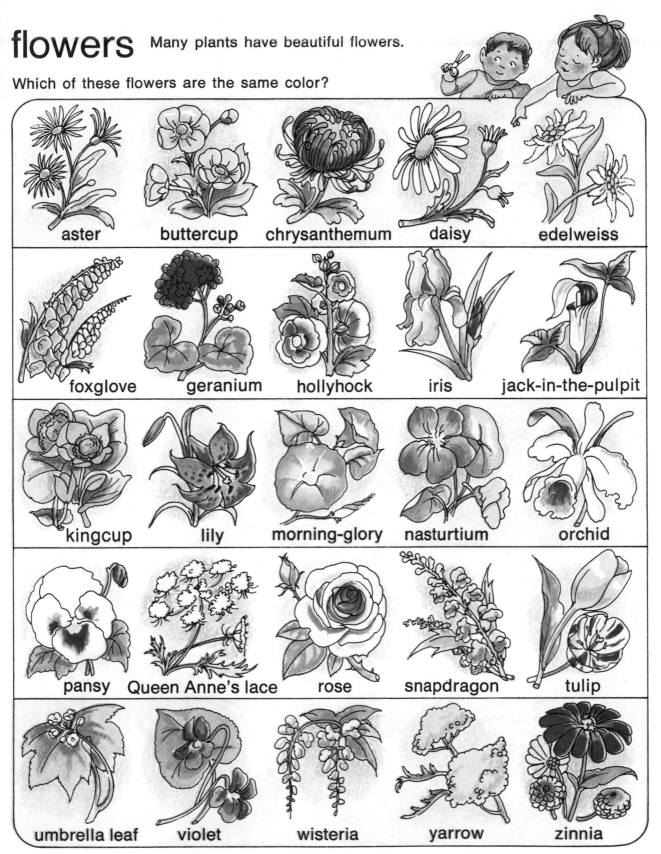

aster	buttercup	chrysanthemum	daisy	edelweiss
foxglove	geranium	hollyhock	iris	jack-in-the-pulpit
kingcup	lily	morning-glory	nasturtium	orchid
pansy	Queen Anne's lace	rose	snapdragon	tulip
umbrella leaf	violet	wisteria	yarrow	zinnia

Which flowers would you like to pick for a bouquet?

food

We eat food to keep our bodies healthy and to help us grow.

Do you eat some of these foods each day?

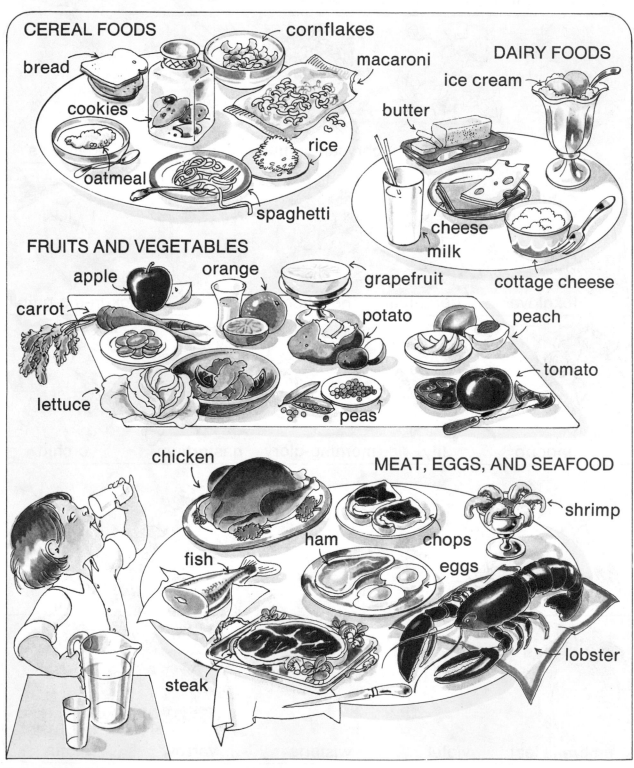

CEREAL FOODS

cornflakes

bread

macaroni

cookies

rice

oatmeal

spaghetti

DAIRY FOODS

ice cream

butter

cheese

milk

cottage cheese

FRUITS AND VEGETABLES

apple

orange

grapefruit

carrot

potato

peach

tomato

lettuce

peas

chicken

MEAT, EGGS, AND SEAFOOD

shrimp

ham

chops

fish

eggs

lobster

steak

Do you drink lots of fresh water too?

Some foods are bubbly.
cola
ginger ale
soda

Some foods are crispy.
celery
cabbage
radishes

Some foods are crunchy.
crackers
nuts
popcorn

Some foods are salty.
olives
potato chips
pretzels

Some foods are smooth.
pudding
gelatin
ice cream

Some foods are sour.
dill pickles
lime
lemon

Some foods are spicy.
chili sauce
ketchup
spiced pears

Some foods are sticky.
honey
peanut butter
jelly

Some foods are sweet.
candy
pie
doughnuts

What are your favorite foods?

F
f

forest

A forest is full of trees.
Other plants and animals live there too.

Some big trees are cut for lumber.

spruce tree

fir tree

flying squirrel

New trees are planted.

sawmill

boards

logs

white-tailed deer

nuthatch

crossbill

lumberjack

sawdust

raccoon

moss   fern   Indian pipe   lady's slipper

Wood from forests can be made into many things.

bowls

cellophane

houses

boxes

furniture

paper
tool handles

fruits

Most fruits are sweet and good to eat.
They grow on plants and have seeds in them.

Some fruits grow on bushes.

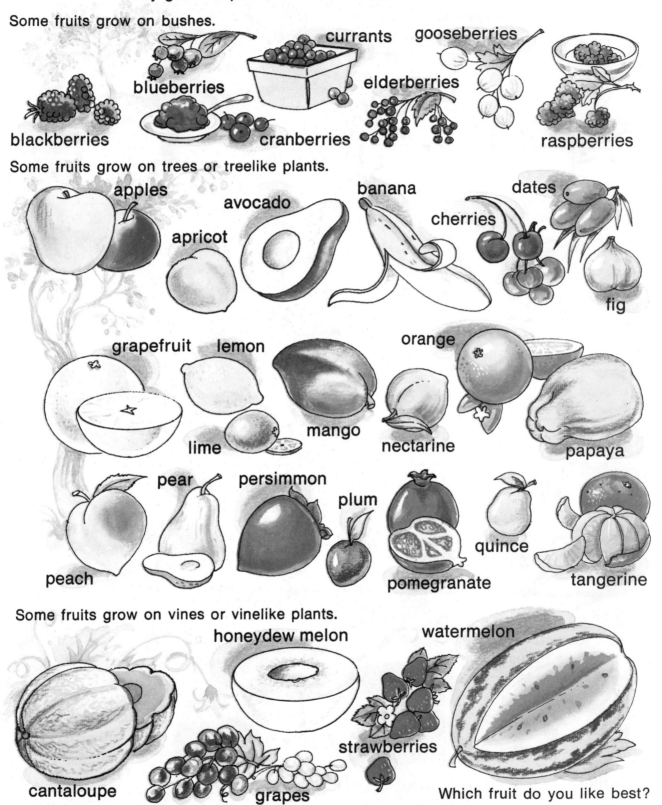

currants

gooseberries

blueberries

elderberries

blackberries

cranberries

raspberries

Some fruits grow on trees or treelike plants.

apples

avocado

banana

dates

apricot

cherries

fig

grapefruit   lemon

orange

lime

mango

nectarine

papaya

pear   persimmon

plum

quince

peach

pomegranate

tangerine

Some fruits grow on vines or vinelike plants.

honeydew melon

watermelon

strawberries

cantaloupe

grapes

Which fruit do you like best?

57

furniture

Furniture makes it comfortable for us to live and work.

We sit on some furniture.

chaise longue

couch

chair

hassock

We sleep on some furniture.

double-decker

bed

canopy bed

cot

We use some furniture for work and play.

easel

table

desk

workbench

We use some furniture to store and hold things.

candlestand

buffet

bureau

chest

serving cart

Gary gives grain to a goose.

ABCDEF **G** HIJKLMNOPQRSTUVWXYZ

These words start with **g**.

gate

geyser

giant   giraffe

girl

glasses

goat

gourds   green grapes   gyroscope

Can you give some girls' names that start with **G**?

abcdef **g** hijklmnopqrstuvwxyz

G
g

games
Which of these games do you like to play with your friends?

checkers

croquet

hide-and-seek

dominoes

jump rope

London Bridge

leapfrog

musical chairs

ring-around-a-rosy

row, row, row your boat

pin the tail on the donkey

What other games do you like to play?

garden

These boys and girls are working in the garden.

scarecrow

Gilbert is hoeing the ground.

trellis

Greg is planting vegetable seeds.

path

BEANS

Glenna is watering her flowers.

Grace is pulling weeds.

wheelbarrow

How do gardeners use these things?

garden gloves

fertilizer

cultivator

hoe

seeds

shovel

rake

spade

trowel

gas station

People buy gasoline at a gas station.
What else do they do there?

GEORGE'S GAS STATION

garage

EXIT

CAR WASH

lift

BATTERY SALE

MAPS

WOMEN MEN

GAS

gas pump

AIR 22 PSI

attendant

ENTER

Can you find these things in the gas station picture?

battery   credit card   oil   map   squeegee

Hans hugs his horse.

ABCDEFG H IJKLMNOPQRSTUVWXYZ

Can you hear the H at the beginning of these words?

hamburger

hawk

headset   helmet

hinge

hole

holly

hook

horn

horseshoe

hummingbird

hyacinth

How many more h words can you name?

abcdefg h ijklmnopqrstuvwxyz

hands

I have
two hands
at the ends
of my arms
to help me
hold things.

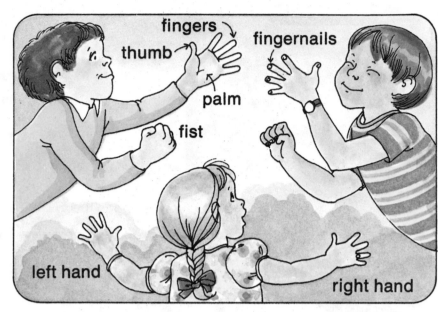

fingers
thumb
fingernails
palm
fist
left hand
right hand

We feel with our hands.
How do these things feel?
Which of them are safe to touch?

prickly
cold
hot
rough
slippery
smooth
hard
soft
wet

Which of these things can you hold in one hand?

book   cat   handkerchief lollipop   purse   telephone

We can do many other things with our hands.

break

build

button

carry

clap

cut

draw

paint

pin

point

shake

tie

wash

wipe

write

zip

Which of these do you wear on your hands?

bandages   gloves   mittens   muff   nail polish   rings

H h

head

Your head is the part of your body that sits on your neck. It has a brain inside so you can think.

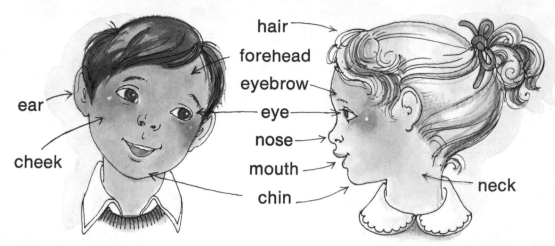

hair
forehead
eyebrow
eye
nose
mouth
chin

ear
cheek

neck

You have two ears to hear with,

You have two eyes to see,

You have a mouth to talk with

And smile so happily.

You have a nose to smell with,

And teeth with which to chew;

A tongue to taste your food with,

Oh, aren't you glad you're you!

Most people have hair on their heads. What kind of hair do you have?

black hair   blond hair   brown hair   curly hair

long hair   mustache   no hair   pigtails

red hair   short hair   straight hair   whiskers

Which of these things do you wear on your head?

bathing cap   beret   bonnet   cowboy hat   earmuffs

football helmet   hair bow   horns   lady's hat   man's hat

rain hat   scarf   stocking cap   sunglasses   wig

Hh

holidays

Each year we celebrate special days.
These special days are holidays.

NEW YEAR'S DAY

horn

confetti

streamers

VALENTINE'S DAY

lace

heart

valentine

APRIL FOOLS' DAY

KICK ME

KICK ME

SAINT PATRICK'S DAY

shamrock

ARBOR DAY

tree

EASTER

chocolate bunny

jellybeans

present

MOTHER'S DAY

bouquet

chick

Easter basket

Easter eggs

FATHER'S DAY

FOURTH OF JULY

fireworks

flag

HALLOWEEN

mask

witch

ghost

jack-o'-lantern

costume

black cat

THANKSGIVING DAY

turkey

CHRISTMAS

star

Christmas tree

candy cane

lights

stockings

angel

Santa Claus

ornaments

CHANUKAH

Menorah
yarmulka

dreidel

homes

A home is where a family lives.

Animal families live in many different kinds of homes.

anthill	aquarium	barn	basket
beaver lodge	beehive	birds' nest	birdhouse
cave	hollow tree	hornets' nest	pouch
shell	tunnel	web	wormhole

apartment house

penthouse

terrace

balcony

People build homes to protect their families. They often use materials they find nearby.

adobe house

cave

glass house

grass hut

houseboat

log cabin

hogan

igloo

mobile home

paper house

stilt house

stone house

tent

tepee

wooden house

house

Most families live in houses. They call their houses homes.

antenna

attic windows

chimney

roof

ceiling

shutters

wall

door window

garage

window box

driveway

porch   shrubs   steps

walk

mud puddle

Some houses have basements underground.

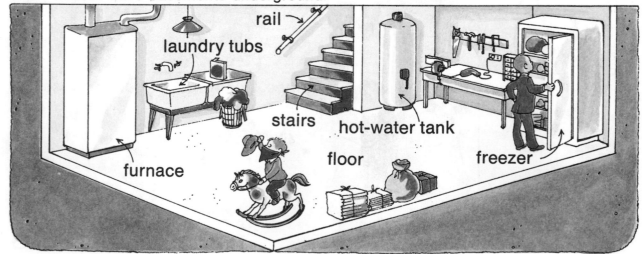

rail

laundry tubs

stairs   hot-water tank

freezer

furnace   floor

72

Isabel is ironing.

ABCDEFGH I JKLMNOPQRSTUVWXYZ

I is the first letter in these words.

ibex

iceberg   icicles   igloo

iguana

impala

incense

inchworm

incubator

iodine

island

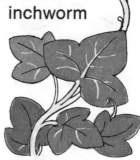
ivy

Look for more **i** words in the Index.

abcdefgh i jklmnopqrstuvwxyz

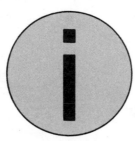

73

Indians

Indians were the first people in America.

These Indians lived on the Great Plains.

hunters

buffalo

chief

Indian pony

tepee

medicine man

papoose

travois

There are many different Indian tribes. They make many beautiful and useful things.

blankets

baskets

dolls

drums

jewelry

moccasins

peace pipe

pottery

totem pole

74

insects

Insects are animals with six legs. Most of them have wings.

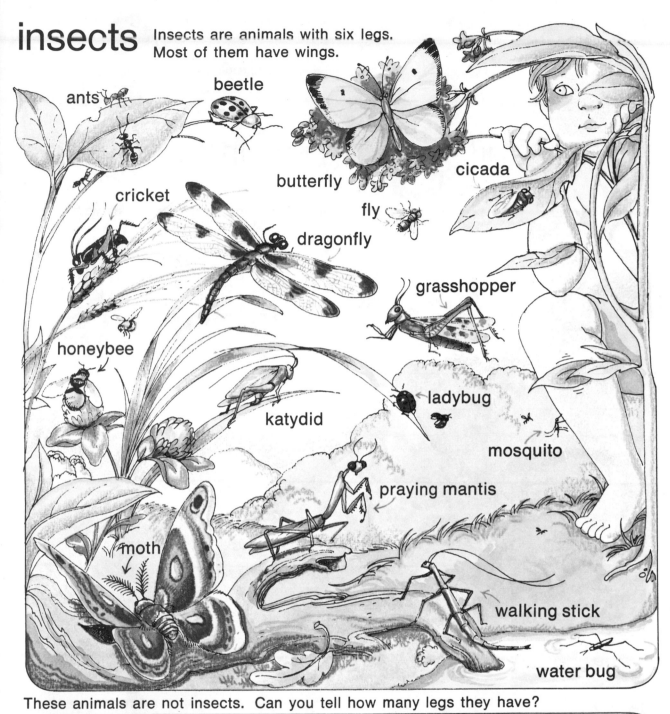

ants

beetle

butterfly

cicada

fly

cricket

dragonfly

grasshopper

honeybee

katydid

ladybug

mosquito

praying mantis

moth

walking stick

water bug

These animals are not insects. Can you tell how many legs they have?

centipede

daddy longlegs

house spider

scorpion

Jeffrey jumps for joy.

ABCDEFGHI **J** KLMNOPQRSTUVWXYZ

Here are some words that start with **J**.

jack

jackknife

jail

janitor

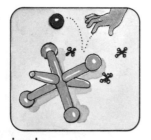

jars

jeep

jellybeans

jester

jockey

jonquil

jug

jumping jack

Can you think of just two more **j** words?

abcdefghi **j** klmnopqrstuvwxyz

76

jungle

A jungle is a hot, wet forest. Trees grow tall to reach the sunlight.

Find these animals and plants in the picture.

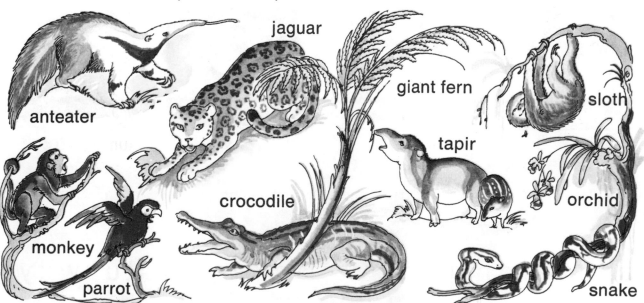

anteater

jaguar

giant fern

sloth

tapir

monkey

crocodile

orchid

parrot

snake

Karen kisses a kitten.

ABCDEFGHIJ **K** LMNOPQRSTUVWXYZ

These words begin with **K**.

kangaroo

kayak

kennel

kettle

key

kimono

king

kite

knight

knitting

knot

kookaburra

How many **k** animals do you think a king might keep?

abcdefghij **k** lmnopqrstuvwxyz

78

kitchen

Our kitchen is a busy place. Mother cooks and bakes in it.
We eat in our kitchen.

cupboard

refrigerator

spice rack

electric mixer

toaster

teakettle

coffeepot

dishwasher

oven

sink

spoon

mug

fork

napkin

place mat

knife

stool

table

We use these dishes when we eat.

sugar bowl and cream pitcher

glass

plate

salt and pepper shakers

cup and saucer

teapot

Mother uses these for cooking and baking.

cake pan

double boiler

juicer

cupcake pan

frying pan

measuring spoons

roaster

soup ladle

mixing bowls

mixing spoon

pie pan

rolling pin

spatula

Laura licks a lollipop.

ABCDEFGHIJK L MNOPQRSTUVWXYZ

Look! Lots of words begin with the letter L.

ladle

lamb

lamp

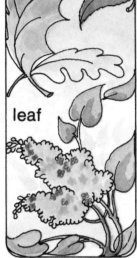

leaf

lei lemonade

letter

lilac

lipstick

lock

locomotive

lynx

Which l words do you like to listen to?

a b c d e f g h i j k l m n o p q r s t u v w x y z

80

Let's pretend.

Sometimes it is fun to dress up and pretend to be other people.

ballerina

bride

veil

train

baby

top hat

magic wand

crown

detective

cape

princess

sailor

magician

Sometimes it is fun to pretend to be animals.

duck

rabbit

elephant

snake

living room

Our family likes to gather in the living room.

drapes

picture

mirror

armchair

table

television

rocker

mantel

rug

fireplace

pillow

sofa

coffee table

Find these things in the living room.

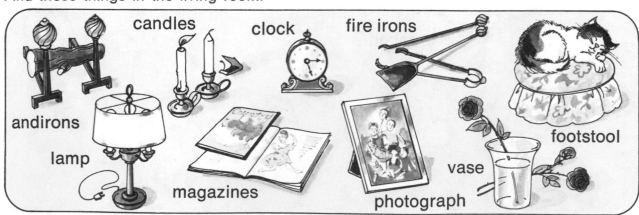

candles

clock

fire irons

andirons

lamp

magazines

photograph

vase

footstool

82

Mike makes music on his mandolin.

ABCDEFGHIJKL M NOPQRSTUVWXYZ

M is in the middle of the alphabet.

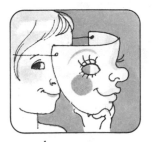

mask

matches

measles

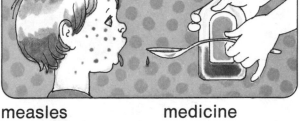

medicine

mittens

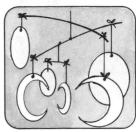

mobile

monkey

money

moon

motorcycle

mouse

mumps

How many more **m** words do you know?

abcdefghijkl m nopqrstuvwxyz

M
m
machines
Machines help us do work. Many machines have wheels.

Can you find the wheels on these machines?

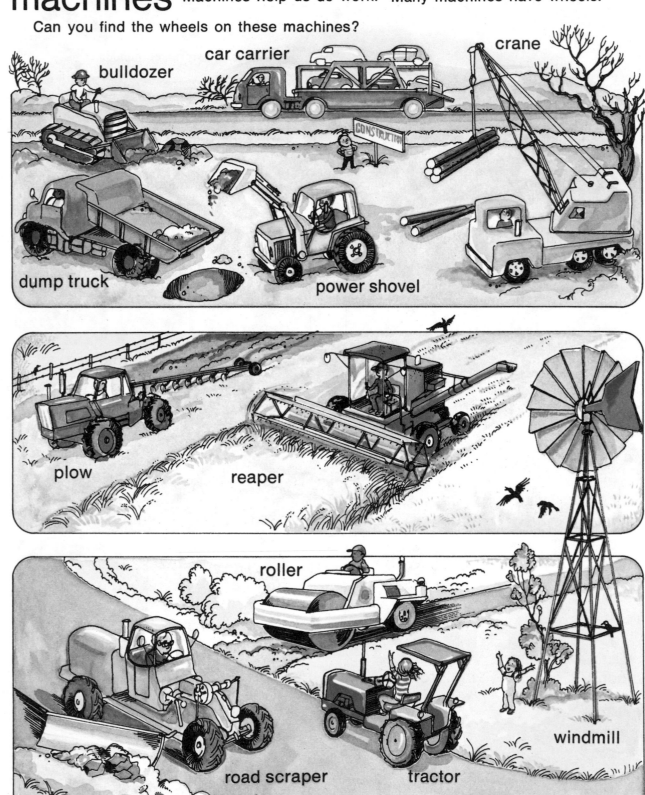

bulldozer

car carrier

crane

dump truck

power shovel

plow

reaper

roller

road scraper

tractor

windmill

Some machines are run by electricity.   How do these machines help us?

drill

sewing machine

air conditioner

iron

blender

dryer

mixer

vacuum cleaner

typewriter

washing machine

dehumidifier

Here are some little machines. Which ones do you know how to use?

can opener

pencil sharpener

eggbeater

nutcracker

scissors

stapler

M m

mail

We send letters and packages through the mail.

mailbox

Mark writes a letter to Morris.
He puts a stamp on the envelope.

Mark mails the letter.

postbox

At the post office the mail is sorted.
The stamps are canceled.
Mark's letter is put in another sack.

post office

A mailman puts the letter in a big sack.
He puts the sack in his truck
and takes it to the post office.

Now Mark's letter travels to a faraway city.

airplane

train

trucks

mailbag

A postman delivers Mark's
letter to Morris.

What do you think the letter says?

manners

If you are courteous to other people you have good manners.

Here are some ways to be courteous.

Shake hands when you meet someone new.

How do you do?

Be quiet when someone is sleeping.

S-h-h-h-h

Let your sister have a turn on the swing.

Thank you

Share your candy with your brother.

Thank you

If you need help or want something, ask politely.

Please

If you accidentally hurt someone, be sure to apologize.

I'm Sorry

medical center

Many sick people go to the
medical center to get well.
Well people go for checkups so
they will stay strong and healthy.

sunroom

nurse

new babies

mother

eye doctor

crutches

broken leg

dentist

x ray

laboratory

doctor

VISITORS

Emergency
Entrance

OFFICES

HOSPITAL

mountain

Mountains are very high hills.
They are made of rock.
Some people live on mountains.

eagle snow peak

glacier

timberline

foothill

shelter

valley

lake

village meadow

mountain climbers

river

hikers

bighorn sheep

waterfall campsite

How would the people in the picture use these things?

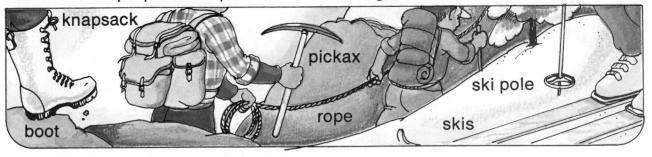

knapsack

pickax

ski pole

rope

skis

boot

museums

Many wonderful things are cared for in museums.
We can go there to see them.

armor

jewelry

ART MUSEUM

furniture

paintings

pottery

sculpture

tapestries

arrowheads

costumes

HISTORY MUSEUM

covered wagon

swords

mummy

old map

The things we see in museums are called exhibits.
Which exhibit do you like best?

ancient animal bones

MUSEUM
OF
NATURAL
HISTORY

fish

butterflies

crystals

plants

rocks

LUNAR ROCK

stuffed animals

MUSEUM OF SCIENCE
AND TECHNOLOGY

airplane

antique automobile

clocks

12:30

rocket

steam locomotive

submarine

M
m

music

Do you like to listen to music?
These musicians enjoy playing together.

conductor

orchestra

Which of these instruments are the musicians playing?

bells

banjo

cello

cymbals

drum

flute

harmonica

harp

double bass

guitar

piano

saxophone

triangle

tambourine

trombone

tuba

violin

When you hear gay music, do you want to dance and sing?

Nancy needs a nap.

ABCDEFGHIJKLM  OPQRSTUVWXYZ

The names of these objects begin with N.

nails

napkins

necklace

needle

nest

net

newspaper

nine nickels

noodles

notebook

nutcracker   nuts

Can you think of nine nice new n words?

abcdefghijklm n opqrstuvwxyz

names

We have names so people will know who we are.
What is your name?

Arthur
Bruce
Corinne
David
Erika
Francisco

Gloria
Helen
Isaac
Jennifer
Kenneth
Lorena
Mary

Norman
Olivia
Patricia
Queen
Ralph
Steven

Tina
Ulysses
Vivian
William
Xavier
Yosuf
Zarita

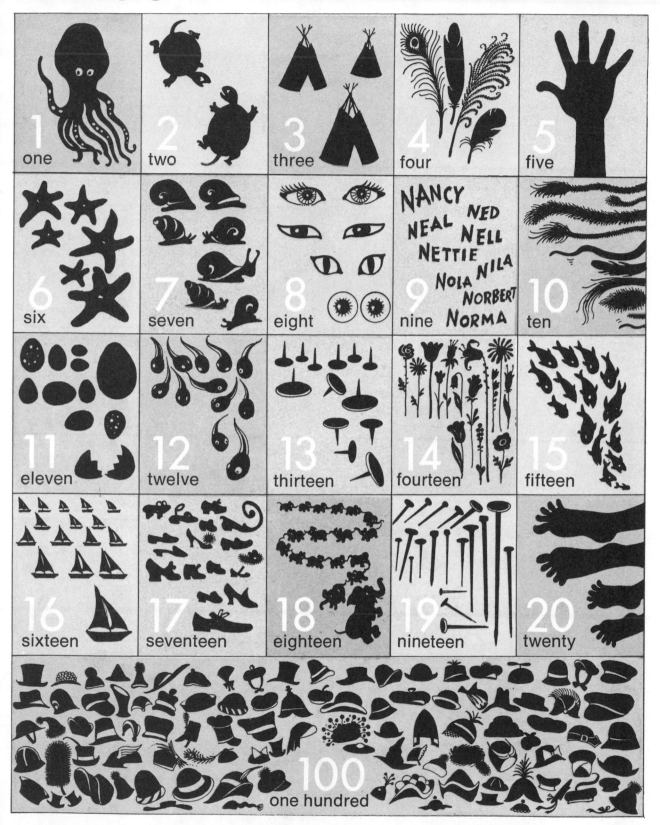

numbers

Numbers tell us how many.

1 one
2 two
3 three
4 four
5 five
6 six
7 seven
8 eight
9 nine
10 ten
11 eleven
12 twelve
13 thirteen
14 fourteen
15 fifteen
16 sixteen
17 seventeen
18 eighteen
19 nineteen
20 twenty
100 one hundred

Oliver owns an octopus.

ABCDEFGHIJKLMN O PQRSTUVWXYZ

These words start with O.

oboe

oilcan

olive

one onion

orange

organ

ostrich

otter

overalls

owl

ox

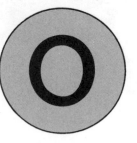

oyster

Can you think of some other O words?

abcdefghijklmn O pqrstuvwxyz

96

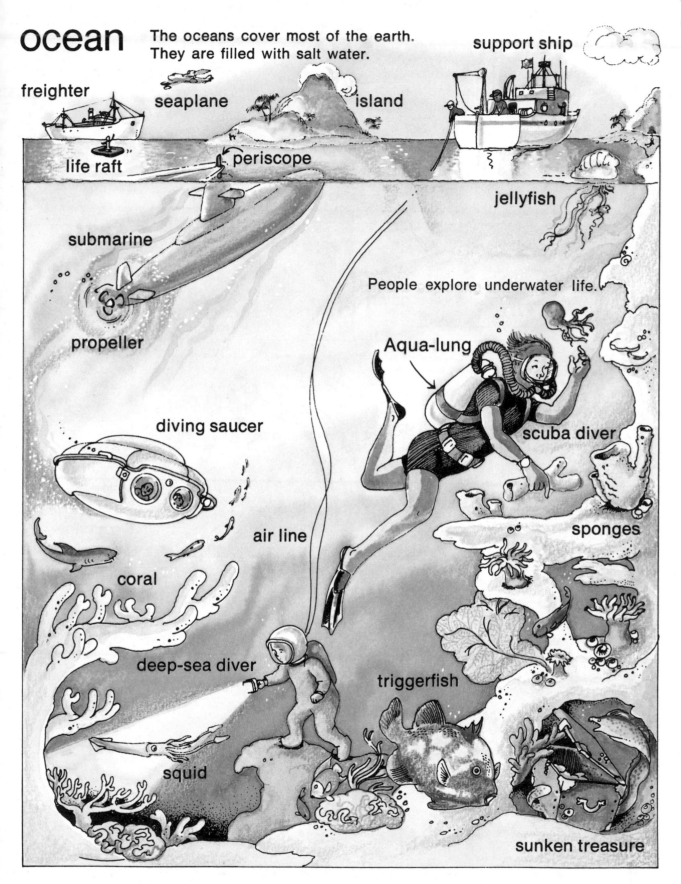

ocean

The oceans cover most of the earth. They are filled with salt water.

freighter

seaplane

island

support ship

life raft

periscope

jellyfish

submarine

propeller

People explore underwater life.

diving saucer

Aqua-lung

scuba diver

air line

sponges

coral

deep-sea diver

triggerfish

squid

sunken treasure

Oo

opposites

When things are altogether different, we say that they are opposite each other.

up

down

high

low

top

bottom

on

off

over

under

inside

outside

upside-down

right side up

left

right

push

pull

old new

happy sad

asleep awake

stop go

tall short

fat thin

in out

come go

ENTRANCE EXIT KINDERGARTEN

HELLO GOODBYE

O o

99

Pamela pets her puppy.

ABCDEFGHIJKLMNO  QRSTUVWXYZ

The words on this page begin with the letter P.

pans

parachute

paste

peacock

peanut

pelican

penny

pepper

pink pig

pizza

plastic pitcher

porpoise

Can you pick out some words that have the letter p in the middle?

abcdefghijklmno p qrstuvwxyz

park

People like to go to the park to relax and play.

Pam and Penny are playing hopscotch.
Paul and Peter are playing tag.
What are the other people doing?

swings

Jungle gym

sidewalk

slide

seesaw

tricycle

statue

tag

hoop

squirrels

pigeons

park bench

fountain

hopscotch

scooter

What do you like to do in the park?

101

P
p

pets
Pets are special animal friends.

Which of these pets would you like for your friend?

canary

cat

fish

mouse

parakeet

hamster

dog

gerbil

snake

pony

turtle

Which of these things would you use to take care of the pets you chose?

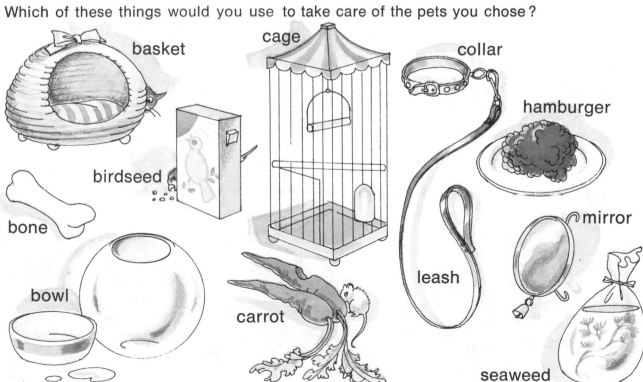

basket

cage

collar

hamburger

birdseed

bone

mirror

bowl

leash

carrot

seaweed

P p

plants

There are many kinds of plants in the world.

They are different shapes and different sizes.

Trees are the biggest plants.

Some plants are so tiny that we need a microscope to see them.

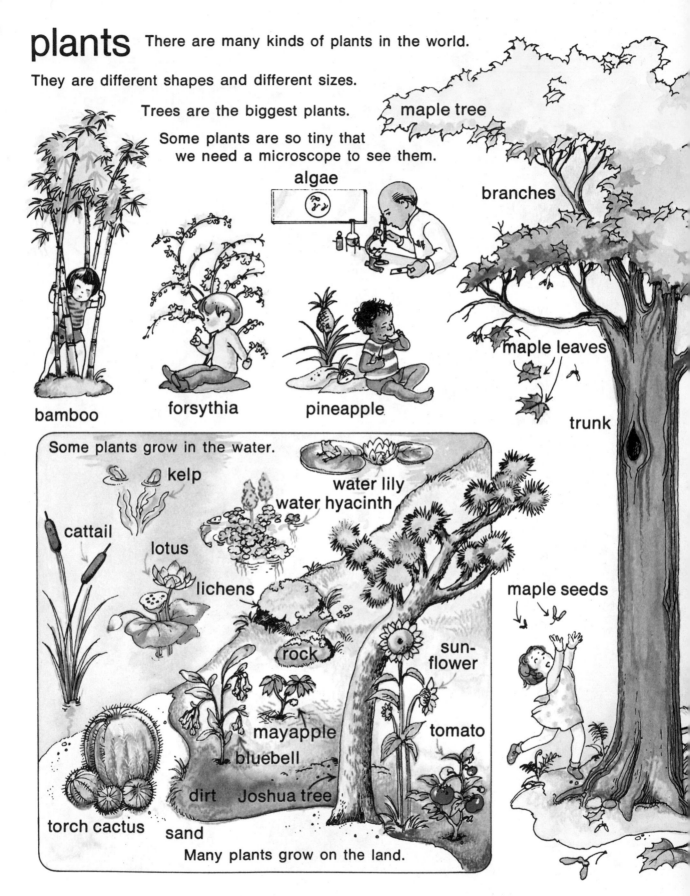

maple tree

branches

algae

maple leaves

trunk

bamboo

forsythia

pineapple

Some plants grow in the water.

kelp

cattail

lotus

lichens

water lily
water hyacinth

rock

sun-
flower

mayapple

bluebell

maple seeds

tomato

dirt   Joshua tree

torch cactus   sand

Many plants grow on the land.

Most plants are green.
Sunshine helps them manufacture
their own food.

Some plants are not green.
They get their food from other plants.

green leaves

flower

fruit

stem

Pepper Plant

roots

coconut palm

cup fungus

shelf fungus

puffballs

mushroom

Indian pipe

chard

clover

club moss

crocus

dandelion

pine tree

pine needles

pine cones

Plants provide food for animals.

nectar

grass

nuts

tree bark

berries

seeds

Can you find more plants in this book?

pond

A pond is a small, shallow lake. It is water with land all around. Many plants and animals grow around the pond.

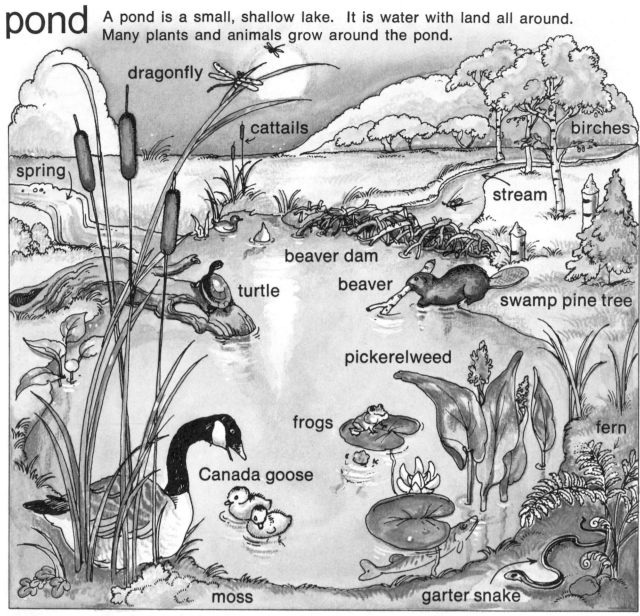

dragonfly

cattails

birches

spring

stream

beaver dam

beaver

swamp pine tree

turtle

pickerelweed

fern

frogs

Canada goose

moss

garter snake

Many plants and animals grow underwater too.

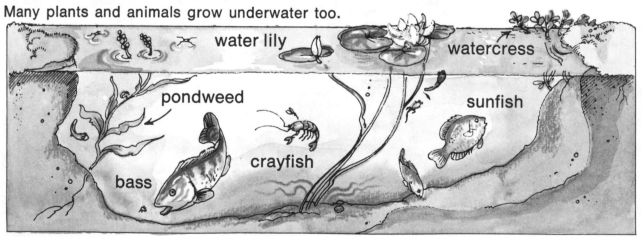

water lily

watercress

pondweed

sunfish

crayfish

bass

prairie

The prairie is flat, rolling glassland. Not many trees grow there.

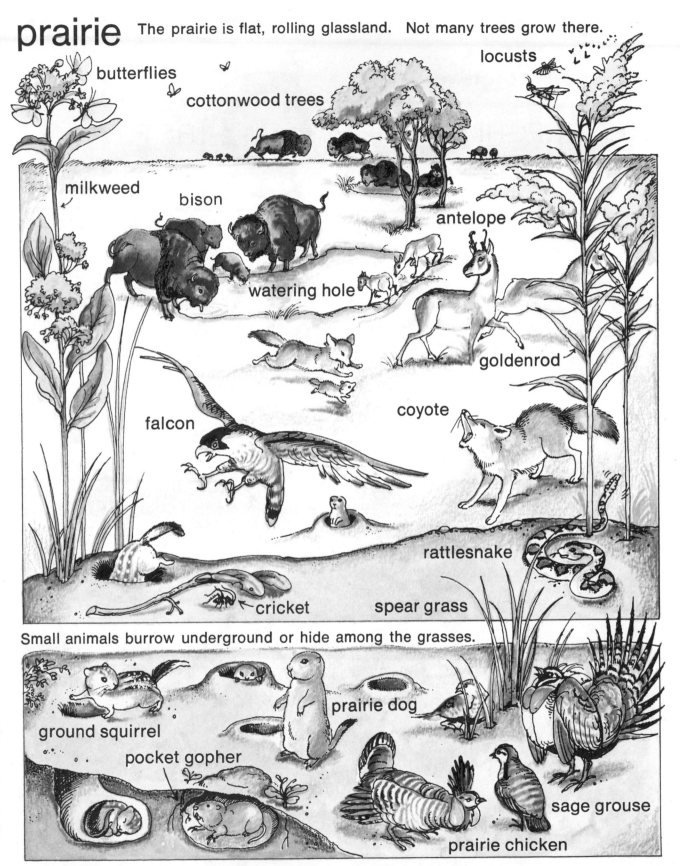

locusts

butterflies

cottonwood trees

milkweed

bison

antelope

watering hole

goldenrod

falcon

coyote

rattlesnake

cricket

spear grass

Small animals burrow underground or hide among the grasses.

prairie dog

ground squirrel

pocket gopher

sage grouse

prairie chicken

107

Quentin quarters a quince.

ABCDEFGHIJKLMNOP Q RSTUVWXYZ

These words begin with Q.

quahog

quail

quarry

quart

queen

questions

quetzal

quill

quilt

quirt

quiver

quoits

Did you notice that q is always followed by U?

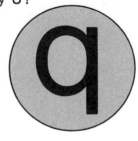

abcdefghijklmnop q rstuvwxyz

108

Ruth rides in a rowboat on the river.

ABCDEFGHIJKLMNOPQ R STUVWXYZ

Can you read these words that begin with R?

raccoon

radish

raisins

rake

record

red ribbon

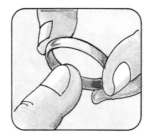

ring

rooster

rope

rose

rug

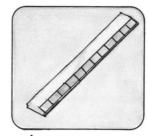

ruler

Which of the words end with r?

abcdefghijklmnopq r stuvwxyz

109

R
r

ranch

A ranch is a very large farm.
Ranchers raise cattle and horses.

bunkhouse

barbecue

cattle

corral

branding cattle

cowboy

chuck wagon

dog

Find these things in the picture.

branding iron

barbed-wire fence

boots

calf

cow

cowgirl

chaps

cow pony

neckerchief

spurs

lasso

ten-gallon hat

R r

windmill

water hole

ranch house

rancher

Would you like to compete at a rodeo?

riding a wild horse

jumping from horse to horse

roping steers

rope tricks

shooting contest

Rodeo Today

R r

reading

Sometimes we read for pleasure.
Sometimes we read for information.

Can you tell why these people are reading?

billboard

clock

cookbook

dictionary

letter

magazine

menu

newspaper

price tag

skywriting

thermometer

traffic light

Ronald's baby-sitter is reading to **him** from his favorite book.

Which of these books do you think Ronald likes best?

Which book
do you like best?

113

R r

river

A river is a large stream of water that flows to the sea.

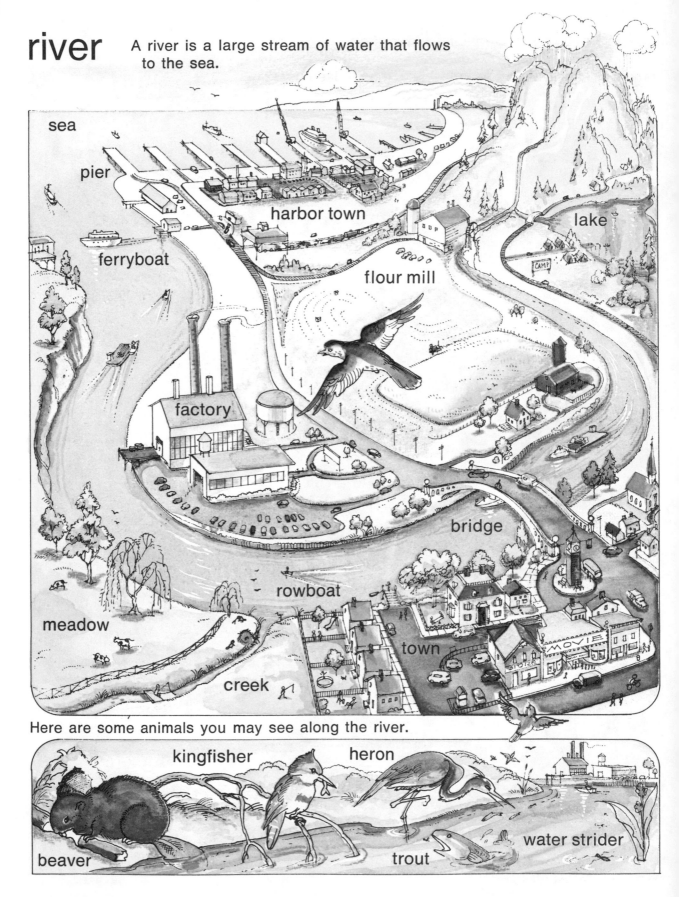

sea

pier

ferryboat

harbor town

flour mill

lake

factory

bridge

rowboat

meadow

town

creek

Here are some animals you may see along the river.

kingfisher

heron

beaver

trout

water strider

Sam sings a silly song.

ABCDEFGHIJKLMNOPQR TUVWXYZ

See all the words that start with S.

safe

satellite

seven seashells

shoes

six spoons

skeleton   skunk

snowman

snowmobile   stagecoach

string

sun

Can you think of several more S words?

abcdefghijklmnopqr tuvwxyz

115

school
Boys and girls go to school to learn.

flag

playground

pupils

What are the boys and girls in this school classroom doing?

globe

goldfish

bookshelves

teacher

plants

dollhouse — blocks

puzzle

Some children walk to school.   Some children ride.

crossing guard

STOP

SCHOOL BUS

more pupils

What do you think these boys and girls are learning?

bulletin board

NEW ZOO BABY

chalkboard

easel

clay

table   crayons

book

paints

seashore

Land by the sea is called the seashore.

bathhouse
lifeguard
beach buggy
sand castle

Which of these things would you take to the beach?

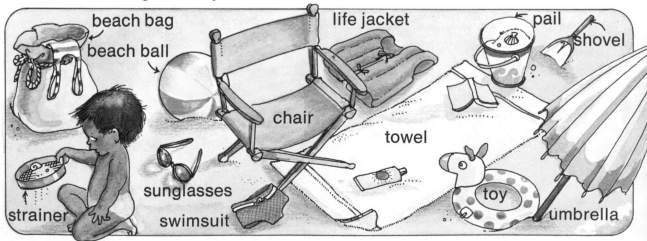

beach bag
beach ball
life jacket
pail
shovel
chair
towel
sunglasses
swimsuit
strainer
toy
umbrella

sky

sun

cloud

lighthouse

ship

ocean

waves

sailboats

surfer

sea grass

Have you ever seen these animals at the seashore?

clams

crab

fish

oyster

lobster

sand dollar

shrimp

sandpiper

sea gull

shells

starfish

seasons

There are four **seasons** in each year.

In many parts of the world the weather **changes** with the seasons.

WINTER

SPRING

AUTUMN

SUMMER

What do you do each season of the year?

shapes

You can cut paper into different shapes.

circle

heart

rectangle

square

star

triangle

What shapes can you find in this picture?

Do you have some blocks shaped like this?

cylinder

rectangular solid

cone

cube

pyramid

prism

sphere

S
s

121

shopping center

What things do you buy in the shopping center?

bank

Books · Records · Cards

department store

bakery

CARPETS

RIDES

barbershop

beauty shop

delicatessen

ENTRANCE

U.S. MAIL

Take-out Orders

LUNCH

theater

variety store

key shop

Laundromat

pet shop

restaurant

shoe store

drugstore

signs

Signs tell us many things.

how far

how fast

how much

what it is

what kind

what to do

when

where

which way

who

What do the signs in this picture tell you?

sizes

The size of a thing is how big it is.

big

little

tiny

long

short

tall

Find the largest and smallest signs in this picture.

S
s

sky
During the day the sky is light.

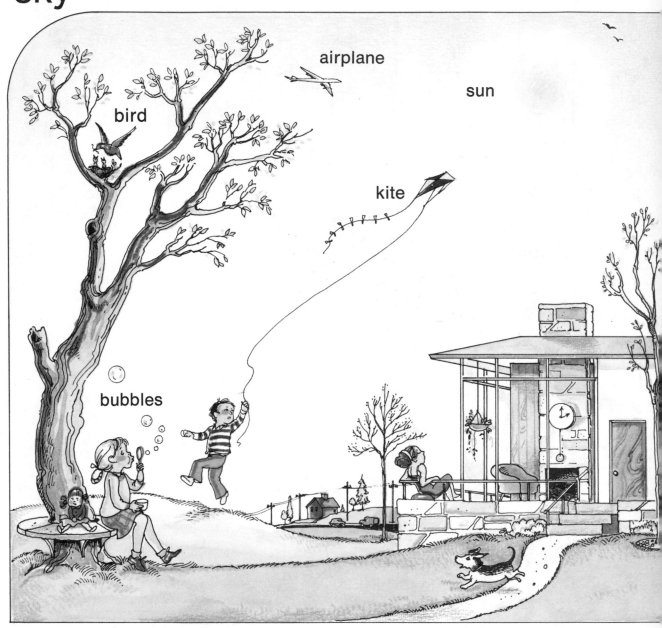

airplane

bird

sun

kite

bubbles

The sun gives us light and heat.

| sunrise | morning | noon | afternoon | sunset |

When night comes the sky gets dark.

bat

owl

telescope

raccoon

opossum

Look for these things in the night sky.

Milky Way   moon   northern lights   planet   stars

sports

Sports are games people play for recreation.

archery

baseball

basketball

bowling

cricket

croquet

fishing

football

golf

How are these balls used in sports?

baseball

basketball

football

golf ball

bowling ball

croquet ball

cricket ball

tennis ball

volleyball

Which are indoor sports? Which are outdoor sports?

hiking

ice-skating

roller-skating

skiing

sledding

swimming

tennis

volleyball

water-skiing

How do the players use these objects?

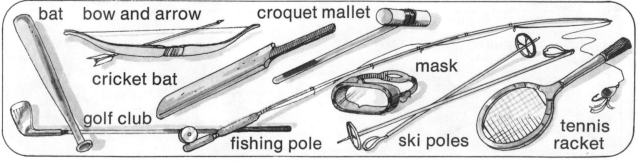

bat   bow and arrow   croquet mallet

cricket bat

mask

golf club

fishing pole   ski poles   tennis racket

129

supermarket

What things do you buy at the supermarket?

HOUSEHOLD SUPPLIES

BAKING SUPPLIES

brooms

mops

OUT

IN

SPECIAL SALE

BAKERY

CANNED GOODS

customers

clerk

candy

FRUIT

check-out counter

VEGETABLES

ONION SPECIALS

Find these things in the picture.

basket

cans

bag

box

OLIVE OIL

cart

MANAGER

DOG AND CAT FOOD

CHEESE

MILK

Eggs

MEAT

butcher

CEREALS

POULTRY

FROZEN FOODS

FISH

cash register

money

purse

scale

tape

Tom talks on the telephone.

ABCDEFGHIJKLMNOPQRS  UVWXYZ

These words start with T.

tambourine

taxi

television

ten triangles

three thimbles

tickets

tired turtle

toboggan

toy train

trunk

two tall trees

twins

Does it tickle your tongue to say t words?

abcdefghijklmnopqrs  uvwxyz

time

Clocks and watches help us tell time.

minute hand

hour hand

cuckoo clock

alarm clock

grandfather clock

electric clock

pocket watch

wristwatch

Here are some other things that help us keep track of time.

calendar

hourglass

sundial

MAY

What time do you do these things?

get up in the morning

eat lunch

watch television

go to bed at night

T t

tools
We use tools to help us get work done.

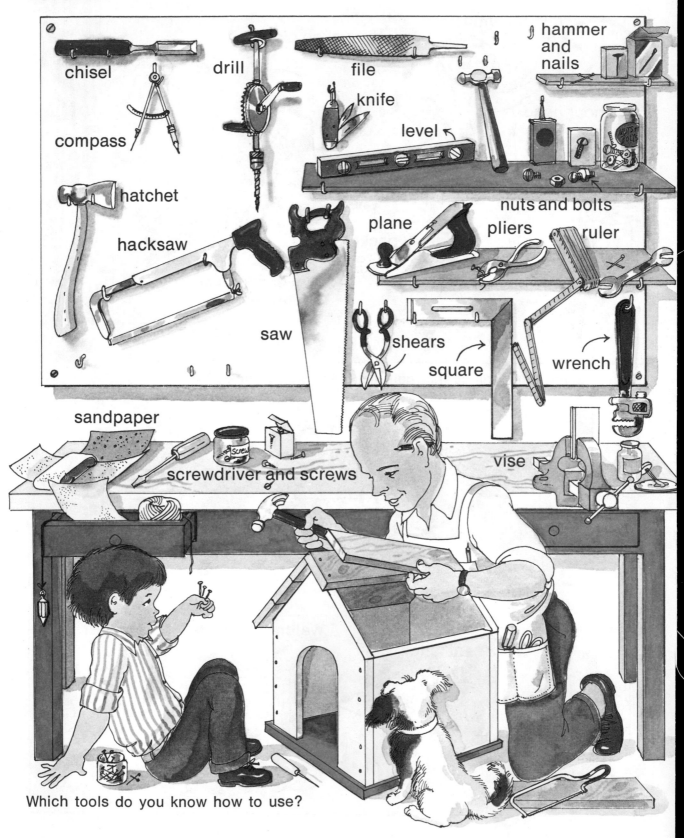

chisel

drill

file

hammer and nails

compass

knife

level

hatchet

nuts and bolts

hacksaw

plane

pliers

ruler

saw

shears

square

wrench

sandpaper

screwdriver and screws

vise

Which tools do you know how to use?

toys

Things we play with are called toys.
Which toys would you like to play with?

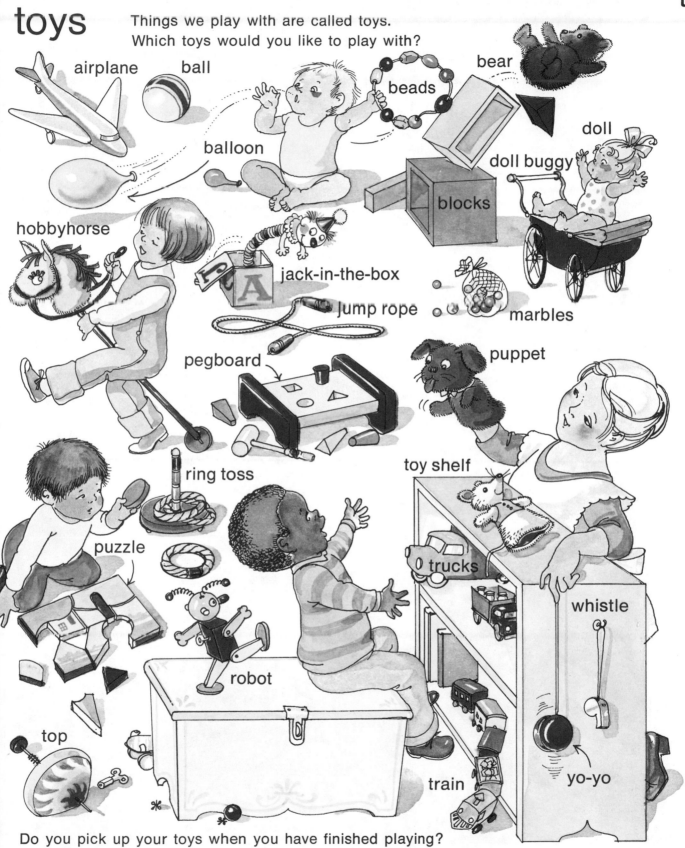

airplane

ball

bear

beads

balloon

blocks

doll

doll buggy

hobbyhorse

jack-in-the-box

jump rope

marbles

pegboard

puppet

ring toss

toy shelf

puzzle

trucks

whistle

robot

top

train

yo-yo

Do you pick up your toys when you have finished playing?

transportation

"Transportation" means carrying people and things from place to place.

Find different ways of traveling on land.

Find different ways of traveling through the air.

Find different ways of traveling on the water.

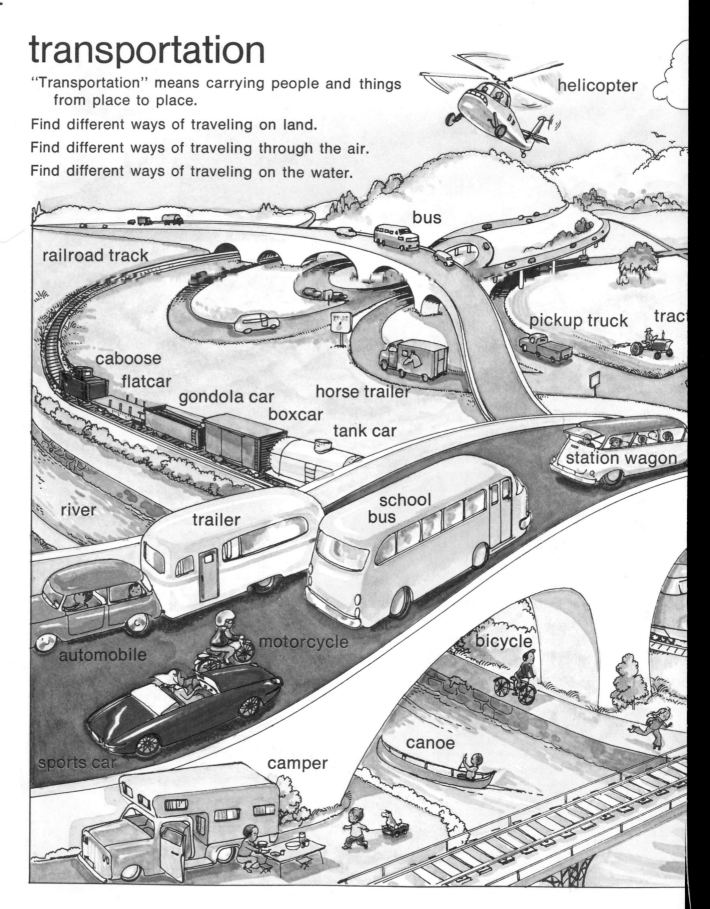

helicopter

bus

railroad track

pickup truck

trac

caboose

flatcar

gondola car

boxcar

horse trailer

tank car

station wagon

river

trailer

school bus

automobile

motorcycle

bicycle

canoe

sports car

camper

blimp

airplane

seaplane

ocean liner

sailboat

bridge

truck

tollbooth

tunnel

taxi

tugboat

train

engine

barge

Ursula uses her umbrella.

ABCDEFGHIJKLMNOPQRST  VWXYZ

Here are some words that begin with U.

ukulele

umbrella

umpire

underwear

unicorn

unicycle

United Nations

United States

upside-down

Can you tell a story using these U words?

abcdefghijklmnopqrst  vwxyz

underground

Many things are happening underground.

Here are some of the things we usually cannot see.

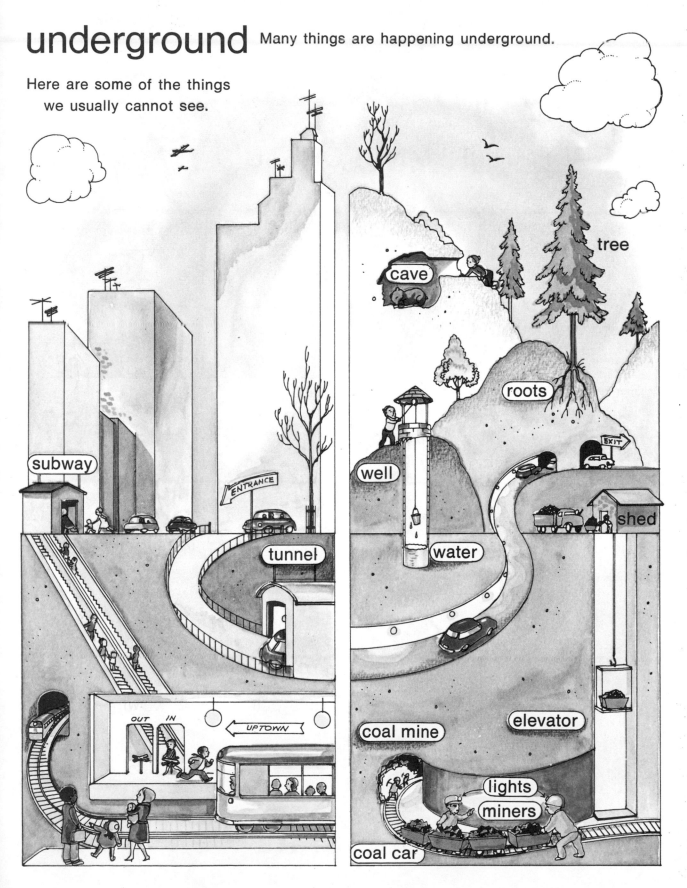

Victor visits Venice.

ABCDEFGHIJKLMNOPQRSTU **V** WXYZ

There aren't very many words that start with **V**.

vacuum cleaner

valentine

vase

vest

vine   violets

violin

vise

vitamins

volcano

volleyball

vulture

Can you think of any more **V** words?

abcdefghijklmnopqrstu **V** wxyz

vegetables
Vegetables are parts of plants we use for food.

Sometimes we eat the leaves.

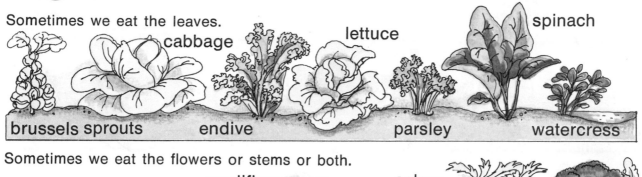

cabbage
lettuce
spinach

brussels sprouts   endive   parsley   watercress

Sometimes we eat the flowers or stems or both.

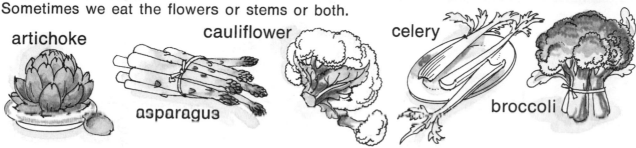

artichoke   cauliflower   celery

asparagus   broccoli

Sometimes we eat the seeds or seed packages.

corn   cucumber   okra

eggplant   lima beans   peas

squash   string beans

peppers   pumpkin   tomato

Many of the vegetables we eat grow underground.

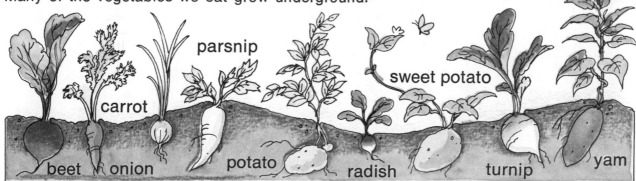

parsnip

carrot   sweet potato

beet   onion   potato   radish   turnip   yam

What vegetables do you like to eat?

Wendy wears a witch's wig.

ABCDEFGHIJKLMNOPQRSTUV  W XYZ

W is the first letter of these words.

wagon   wall

wallet

watch

watermelon

wheel

windmill

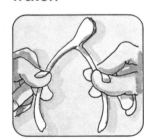

wishbone

wishing well

woodpecker   worm

wreath

Which W words would you like to whisper?

abcdefghijklmnopqrstuv  W xyz

142

weather

The weatherman predicts the weather.

weather map
weather balloon
barometer thermometer
weather vane

Weather changes.

clouds

hurricane

lightning

rain

rainbow

snow

sunshine

tornado

winds

What kind of weather do you have today?

W
w

work

Grown-ups do many different kinds of work.

artist

astronaut

author

baseball player

beautician

bricklayer

computer programmer

dancer

executive

fire fighter

florist

homemaker

garbage collector

librarian

They have many different occupations.

mail carrier

milk carrier

nurse

photographer

mechanic

plumber

sales person

scientist

seamstress

police officer

steelworker

singer

taxi driver

waitress

secretary

What occupation do
you want to have when you grow up?

W
w
world

Here is a map of the world. Most of the world is covered with water.

Joan

Oonark

Alex

Jimmy

ARCTIC OCEAN

Rosita

NORTH
AMERICA

ATLANTIC
OCEAN

Kamehameha

PACIFIC OCEAN

SOUTH
AMERICA

Chela

Kuma

ANTARCTIC
OCEAN

Juanita

Kivi

Roderick

The people of the world are more alike than different.

146

W
w

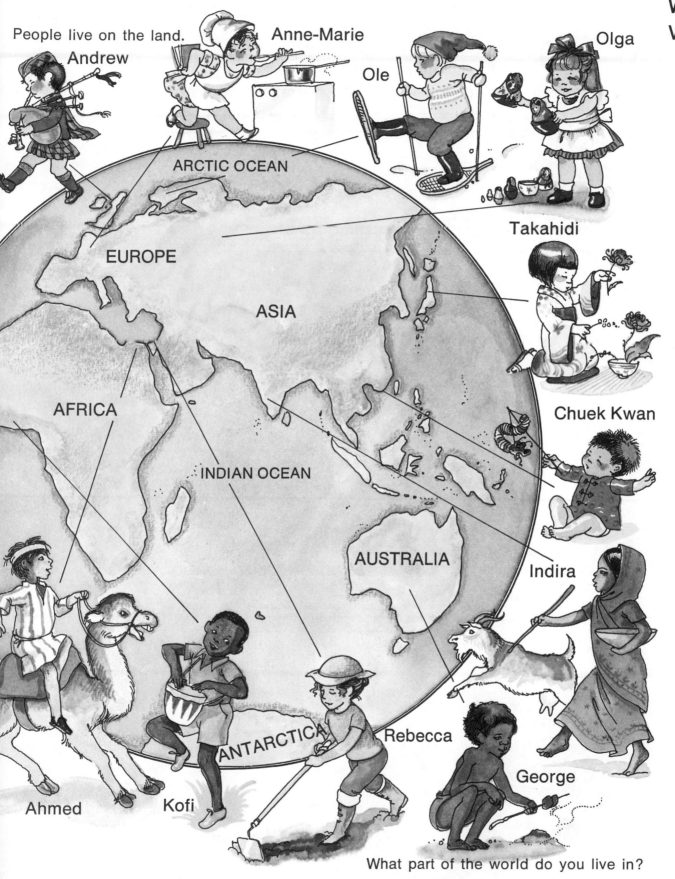

People live on the land.
Andrew
Anne-Marie
Ole
Olga
ARCTIC OCEAN
Takahidi
EUROPE
ASIA
Chuek Kwan
AFRICA
INDIAN OCEAN
Indira
AUSTRALIA
ANTARCTICA
Rebecca
George
Ahmed
Kofi

What part of the world do you live in?

147

W
w

writing

Sometimes we write letters and numbers.
Sometimes we write names.
Sometimes we write messages.

chalk

eraser

magic slate

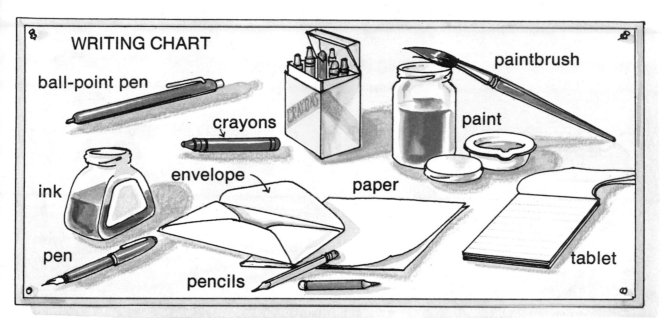

WRITING CHART

ball-point pen

crayons

paintbrush

paint

ink

envelope

paper

pen

pencils

tablet

pencil sharpener

easel

typewriter

desk

chair

What do you write?

Xerxes examines his x ray.

ABCDEFGHIJKLMNOPQRSTUVW**X**YZ

Not many words begin with **X**, but **X** is a special letter.
Can you tell why?

"Xmas" is short for "Christmas."

X marks the spot.

Sometimes "X" means "wrong."

"XXXX" means lots of kisses.

xray

an X sign

xylophone

Can you think of some words that end with **X**?

abcdefghijklmnopqrstuvw**X**yz

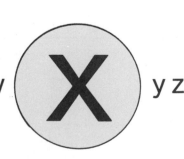

Yetta yells "Yippie-i-yay-i-yay!"

ABCDEFGHIJKLMNOPQRSTUVWX  Z

Here are some words that start with Y.

yacht

yak

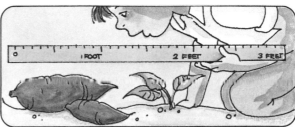
yam   yardstick

yarn

yarrow

yawl

yawn

yellow yolk

yoke

yo-yo

yucca

Can you think of any more y words?

abcdefghijklmnopqrstuvwx  z

Y
y

yard
Do you ever play in the yard?

umbrella table

patio

hose rack

grass

Find these objects in the picture.

birdbath   birdhouse   fence   gate   hose

lawn mower   pool   sandbox   sprinkler   swing

Zoe zips her zipper.

ABCDEFGHIJKLMNOPQRSTUVWXY

Z is the last letter in the alphabet.

Here are some words that begin with **Z**.

zebra

zephyr   zeppelin

zero

zigzag

zinc

zinnia

zipper

zither

zoom

zucchini

Zulu

Which **Z** word might you hear at the zoo?

abcdefghijklmnopqrstuvwxy

Z
z

ZOO

Have you ever been to a zoo? A zoo is like a hotel for animals.
The animals come from many parts of the world.

These animals came from [Africa.]

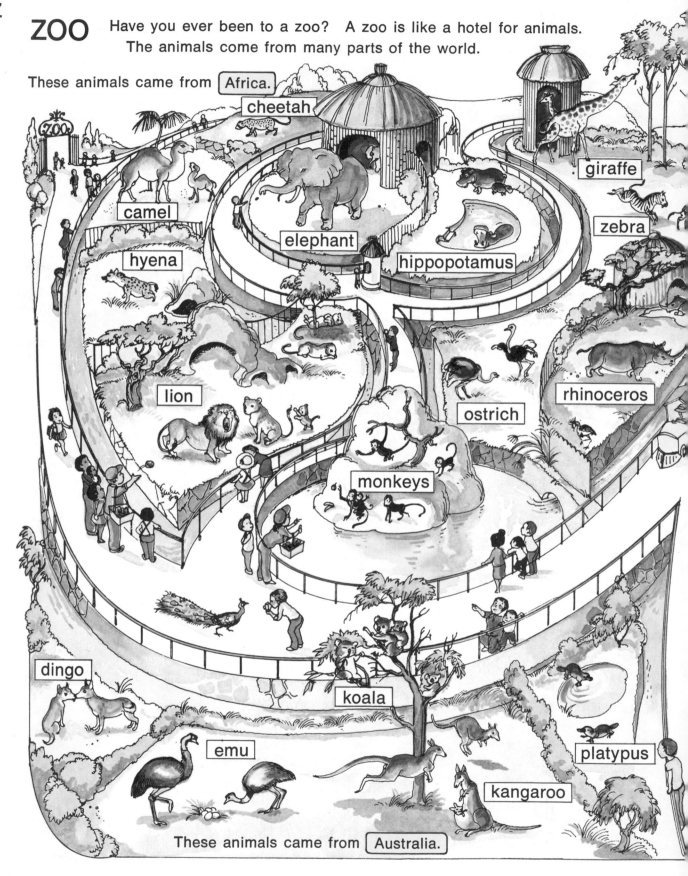

cheetah

giraffe

camel

zebra

elephant

hyena

hippopotamus

lion

rhinoceros

ostrich

monkeys

dingo

koala

emu

platypus

kangaroo

These animals came from [Australia.]

These animals came from **Eurasia.**

chamois

ibex

gazelle

cobra

tiger

polar bear

mongoose

panda

Have you seen these animals from **North America?**

caribou

musk ox

bison

grizzly bear

bobcat

anteater

llama

armadillo

ocelot

penguin

Which of these animals from **South America** do you like best?

155

index

In the index below, you will find words that do *not* appear on the book's 26 Alphabet Pages. (An Alphabet Page is one on which all the words begin with the same letter.)

The names of people are not listed in the index.